PRAISE FOR
DRAWN OUT LOVE!

"In a culture where intense sex and feverish romance is the norm in most gay fiction, *Drawn Out Love!* is a romance of a more classic variety. This is a story where the simple, brave act of taking someone's hand can hold the promise of a happy future."

– Charles "Zan" Christensen
Northwest Press

"I really enjoyed this sweet, old-fashioned love story, which you don't often see in contemporary gay fiction. There was a lot of love in the narrative! It makes you feel romantic and a little jealous about not being Brody or Keith."

- Mark Brill
Magic: The Gathering and fantasy artist

This novel is a work of fiction. Names, characters, places, and incidents are either used fictitiously or are the product of the author's imagination. Any resemblance to actual events or places or persons, living or dead, is entirely coincidental.

DRAWN OUT LOVE!

Published by Bright Horse Publishing.

Distributed by Kindle Direct Publishing.

Artwork by Adam Florian.

facebook.com/drawnoutlove

ISBN-13: 978-057883409-2

First edition: June 2021

10 9 8 7 6 5 4 3 2 1

DRAWN OUT LOVE!

DEREK FAIRBANKS

A BRIGHT HORSE PUBLISHING BOOK

1

MAN, I'D FORGOTTEN WHAT it was like to be kissed!

As we stood there in his hotel room...

Hey! Get your minds out of the gutter. It wasn't like that at all. I guess I should backtrack. My name's Brody Rohan. I write stuff. More specifically, I write sci-fi stuff. Make a pretty decent living at it, actually. Kinda amazing when you consider I spent way too much of my adult life doing the hand-to-mouth thing, but you're not here for an exploration of my economic hang-ups. People like my work, and my bank likes that they like it. Moving on.

So, I was working on my next novel. I wanted to do something about aliens, tying it into the current political climate we're living in. I was almost done when I found out the artist I usually partner with was no longer available. Something to do with him and his new husband packing up and moving to Australia. It happens.

As it also happened, I'd recently begun communicating with this dude I met in a mutual interest social media group. His name is Keith Kirby. I'd liked some of the observations he'd posted and there was no way I wouldn't have noticed the handsome, bearded face staring back at me from his profile pic. Other than that, I didn't know him from a hole in the wall. One thing I did learn before too long is that his artwork is the bomb. Like, a whole arsenal of bombs.

Keith was legit, too. Like I said, I've done well for myself; it's just that he draws for a major publisher. There's no way he'd deign to do some sketches for somebody lower on the food chain, right? And even if he did, I figured he'd probably charge more arms and legs than I was able to part with.

But nothing ventured. At this point we had friended each other and even had a few electronic chats. The least he could say is no, or yes with a reason for *me* to say no. And wouldn't you know! Keith actually came back with a very affordable quote considering the caliber of his work. I told him what I wanted and the end result was really epic. And slightly delayed, with him having to squeeze it in during comic cons and all. I admit I got more than a little antsy as my own publication date got a little too close for comfort. At any rate, I submitted his artwork on time and it was totally the perfect compliment to the story I'd wanted to tell.

That would have been the end of it, I guess. We each had our own lives and our work there was done. Except there was this one night we were online and I was feeling crappy and took a chance on voicing it to him. We don't yet live in a world where you can arbitrarily start talking mental health to just anyone and have it be understood. Amazingly, Keith could empathize and he even opened up to me about some of his own personal struggles. I mean, here I am, a virtual stranger apart from his doing some work for me. I was touched. Not only did I feel like he got me on a very specific level, I felt like that night we moved beyond simple business relationship and began construction on friends.

He took a chance of his own in that same conversation. He came out to me. I don't have to tell you that can be a chancy thing to do, even on the Internet where you don't necessarily have to come face-to-face with anyone. Fortunately, he didn't have anything to worry about with me on that score – birds of a feather and all – and with already some major things in common, I suggested we continue getting to know each other over the next little while. He agreed. Cool!

Of course, you know one other fact of online life. It pours Miracle-Gro on that whole "easier typed than done" thing. Months went by and admittedly I got busy with my own demands, as I presume he did, and said getting to know each other didn't happen. Until one day I got a message from him – he was doing a con a few hours from me in San Francisco. Why didn't we meet in person? Hey, there was an idea! My career didn't always require me to leave my home in Reno that much, so I rather jumped at that chance. All I had to do was drive three-ish hours. We synchronized our day planners, and before long it was the night before our get-together.

But instead of sleeping peacefully, I lay awake, conflicted. What for? This wasn't going to be a big deal. Me author, you illustrator, we grab a cup of coffee, talk shop, shake hands, go our separate ways. It's just that... well, he was so darn cute. Tall. Hazel eyes. Light brown yet graying hair matched by a similarly-hued beard. Slight glint of mischief on his intelligent face.

Okay, truth-or-dare time: I had been single for what

felt like forever. Only four or five years, but, in line with admonishing you to avoid the gutter before, I'm not like most guys. I've never been interested in sleeping around. I mean, you do you, but I like a little love and fidelity with my lovemaking.

Lovemaking. See, that was the conflict. Being such a good boy, it had been eons since I'd engaged in any horizontal tangoing. My ex and I had stopped sleeping together long before we broke up. And I swear, it's like ultimately every guy I get interested in is straight. I was in the middle of what I'd come to call "the drought." No rain, no huggin', no kissin', no nothin' else. You know, you can actually learn to exist in that state? Except I always came back to what I'd once read about babies dying from lack of affection. Bad as that sounds, no hookup app or escort site in the world was worth preventing that fate to me. It's just too scary a world. And if I'm completely honest, I had other reasons for keeping the goodies to myself, too.

So, should I try to bust a move on this guy and remember what that part of myself was even like, or just keep it professional? My phone lit up my dark bedroom as I once again looked at that scruffy face. I let myself fantasize how it would feel to be held, and yes, a few other things. It would probably be a snap to get something going...if it were anyone else but me.

By the time daylight and my departure time arrived, I'd thought better of it. Not! It was *all* I could think about all the way to San Fran, outside of which exit to take and the GPS' directions to his hotel. The suspense got prolonged when he messaged me he was sightseeing with some friends and would I mind meeting a couple hours later. I did mind, but I wasn't going to tell him no. It just meant I had to wander through some stores and nearly kill my phone battery playing games to keep myself occupied. Unfortunately that extra time was just fuel for my doubt. It was silly. I wasn't going to say anything to Keith. It was a dumb idea to begin with.

Finally the anointed hour came. I walked through the lobby of his hotel in more of a daze than I'd really rather admit. I didn't know what to expect, or if I should expect anything. I took a breath getting out of the elevator. Part of me wanted to turn around and go home! But I rose above that and knocked on his door. I made myself, because I knew, once I did that, there was no turning back.

There was a movie quality to the way he was backlit by the setting sun when he opened the door, the way it made him more silhouette than man. But no, he was real – which he didn't know he was proving by greeting me enthusiastically and pulling me into a hug right away. If that didn't help tamp down my nervousness, the ultimate effortlessness of our conversation certainly did. Here I thought there would be these uncomfortable silences punctuating some strained chit-chat about our respective industries. Yet as he sat on the bed (which I admit put a few more salacious thoughts in my head), and I in the chair beside him, we quickly bypassed such formality and started getting into some real nitty-gritties.

It was one thing to find ourselves on the same side where the state of our country was concerned, but then we started talking about our past relationships. Dipping my toe in the water, I even made a joke about "the drought". And I found out he had grown children from his nine-year marriage to a woman. The way we so easily lighted on deeper topics, it was hard to believe this was a fellow I'd only met an hour or so before. He felt like too much of a kindred spirit for that.

It got dark during our confab, making us realize dinner would not be entirely inappropriate. So we Googled some local restaurants and headed down to the one we picked out. On the way, Keith said that it seemed like most gay men simply wanted to have open relationships. And he said it as a lament, not like he was preaching the gospel of them. Look, I've come far enough to acknowledge that if two guys want an open sitch, and it makes them both happy, who am I to criticize. I've just learned the hard way that it isn't for me. See, I had come out of a twelve-year open relationship, but I'd gone into that aspect of it kicking and screaming. My ex didn't want to commit to me sexually and I didn't want to lose him. So I agreed. And I rather boldly told Keith I would rather be alone than go through that again. I just got the feeling Keith himself believed in monogamy, and I couldn't help it – I liked him even more for it.

At dinner, we skated the surface by talking about how he'd settled in Bozeman, Montana and delving into the actual existence of life on other planets, then just as easily got down into the valleys of the ultimate *ish*. I studied Keith's face as he spoke, laughed, ate. At one point this wave came over me. It felt like we were on a first date. The sensation was so strong it was hard to restrain. But we were not on a date, first or fiftieth, and I forced myself to push it down. I was so mixed up! I couldn't decide if I was just having a nice conversation with a like-minded someone...or if there was something else going on. And my hormones were fully short-circuiting.

I took him back to his hotel. I excused myself to the Mother Nature room, but it was just as much to grab a private moment and make some sort of choice as anything else. I wanted him. I wanted Keith. But our four-hour beyond-casual talk had made casual sex even more of an impossibility for me. Hell, who was I kidding – I'd rarely had casual sex, for all the reasons I told you about. Couldn't go through with it then, and I couldn't go through with it now. So what was there to do? I had to go out there, shake his hand, be on my way and keep following him on social media. There was no point to anything else.

I reappeared, and he looked up from his phone. Damn it. Here was this man who so far was a better match than anyone I could have found locally on a dating app, especially the ones chock full of "straight" married men who just wanted to experiment. Keith's smile was so engaging, gentle. How was I supposed to walk away and pretend none of this had happened? How was that living authentically? I know I fumbled over the words, words I deemed the most reasonable compromise I could think of given everything swirling around inside me:

"I just want to say...I think you're adorable."

There! Got that out of my system. I was honest and even a little bit daring, for me, anyway. I could live with that. I tried to make myself turn around and head for the door, but suddenly it was like everything in the room slowed down. Keith didn't say a word. But something had come over his face, something sure, something warm. He stepped forward gingerly and ran his hand through my thick, red, starting-to-gray curly hair. His lips brushed against mine. We melted into a slow, soft kiss. My heart was racing faster than my brain, and I didn't even think that was possible.

Oh, yes, I'd forgotten what it was like to be kissed. But it wasn't merely the moistness of his mouth and the scratch of his whiskers against mine that was exciting me. Because his wasn't one of those I-just-want-to-fuck-you kisses, the ones where you find a tongue shoved down your throat and teeth gnashing against yours. I've had those. This...it was almost...loving. I never wanted it to stop.

Of course it had to, and I felt this intense rush of happiness and sadness at the same time. "I wish you could stay," Keith smiled. I did, too, with every fiber of my being. Unfortunately he had to fly out the first thing in the morning, and I still had a three-plus-hour drive ahead of me that would get me home well after midnight. We reluctantly broke the embrace. I couldn't believe I had finally found someone I had so much in common with. But I told myself it was just one of those soap-like romantic moments that just couldn't be built on.

That's why what he said next was like manna from heaven. He was scheduled to appear at this huge comic con in Baltimore in a couple of months...the same week I was going to be within decent driving distance of him doing a book event at a sci-fi convention in Philadelphia. Why not meet up and pick up where we were leaving off?

There was no way I was going to refuse that suggestion. Instead of having to say goodbye, I was able to leave that hotel room with something to look forward to. I still had to force myself out the door, but I couldn't stop smiling.

I mean the smile was glued to my face all the way back to Reno.

As I put my key in the door of my house, I was half delirious both from exhaustion and adrenaline. I was so glad we didn't end up in bed. That would have rocked, I was sure now, but I didn't just want to have sex – I wanted to make love. And for the first time in what felt like decades, that actually seemed possible. I didn't know how I was going to wait two months to see him. Damn, I didn't even know how I was going to sleep with so many thoughts and feelings and urges rushing through my head and heart and crotch.

They say it happens when you least expect it. Well, this sure as hell fit that definition. Don't worry, I knew – this could go anywhere, or nowhere. But I had to at least thank the universe and be grateful for the experience, whatever did or didn't happen next. I kept touching my lips, as if to connect with Keith and remind myself that his kisses weren't something I'd merely imagined. An easy thing to wonder, sitting in my own bedroom again.

I finally managed to knock out. As I did, I thought that maybe, just maybe, Keith might be the reason I wouldn't ever have to forget what it was like to be kissed again.

2

WELL, AS YOU MIGHT figure, the next day I woke up and it was like none of it happened. Surely I'd dreamt the whole thing. Thankfully, the book with his artwork on the cover that I'd had him autograph was a tangible enough reminder, as was the selfie of us staring at me from my phone. Though in all candor, if it hadn't been for those things there was still that buzzing thrill inside me, the one that said there was at least a possibility of ultimately having someone special in my life after going it alone for so long.

I'd long since passed the rather dysfunctional concept that I had to have a man to feel complete. Yet there's always that void you feel on one level or another, at least for me. I also have a nasty habit of rushing in where angels fear to tread when it comes to *affaires de coeur*. So barely twelve hours after this awesome encounter came reason to not get too ahead of myself. You might as well know it was hard not to. But I had no intention of scaring Keith off with my special brand of enthusiasm. I wanted to come at this, whatever this was, from a healthier place.

I made myself wait 'til late in the afternoon to send him the photo we had taken with "our" book. I was sure we could both use the image for promotion but it was also a none-too-subtle reminder that I was real, in case he had woken up with a similar sense of unreality about it. Keith replied almost instantly, telling me he had enjoyed our meeting and was looking forward to our next one. Short but sweet. I made curbing any major effusiveness seem easy on the surface, but just under that surface it was like trying to keep a wild horse from breaking free.

Over the next few days we messaged some more, and things were super caj. I'm the type of guy that I wanted to talk about what happened back at the hotel and how we might capitalize on it. Instead, nothing we typed out to each other referenced our kisses or even hinted at anything romantic. Just stuff about his delayed flight home, the cold he felt coming on, etc. That was a lead and it behooved me to follow it.

Still, as much as it was nice to cyber-chat with him on a regular basis the week following our meeting, I was getting to a place where I had things to say and needed to say them. Especially since he was going to be travelling to another comic con and could easily be incommunicado for several days. So, though I had to hold my breath a bit – this was going to be the first milepost on Potential Rejection Road – I sat down and wrote him that I liked who I'd met. I liked how we were able to talk about the mundane and the monumental. And since we had eight weeks until our next visit, why not spend that time getting to know each other? That way we would be far less strangers to each other by the time it happened.

I glowed after he wrote back that he was on board with that arrangement. It was a good place to leave things after he flew off to once again meet fans and hawk his wares. I did my best to get on with the business of my own work, errands, what-have-you. But lordy, I thought of him a lot. I hadn't fully let myself acknowledge in recent years that I wanted a real relationship with someone with whom there was mostly equal attraction and intent. See, my ex had been horrible about emotional declarations and I went our dozen years never really knowing if he was in love with me, because he never said it. I'm a words guy. What am I supposed to infer from a lack of words?

Yeah, actions speak louder and all that. But it was unnerving because I'd always sensed that Mr. X wasn't really in love with me, and that on top of the open relationship had eroded my own commitment until finally I just had to face up to what I'd been running from for so long and call it quits. I wanted someone who was as into me as I was into him, and I had learned the hard way how necessary that is. I realized it was way too early to even start thinking about Keith in those terms – I mean, I barely knew the guy. A little fantasy or two, however, wasn't going to hurt anything. I'd come far enough to know it was how I acted in real life that counted.

Finally Keith and I made plans to kick it old school and talk on the phone. I made sure to pick up on the third ring so I didn't seem too eager; in those seconds I tried to think of a way to express my hopes to him without being overwhelming – as if I hadn't spent the past few days trying to navigate that exact balance. Hearing Keith's voice again...it had been a couple of weeks and the seductive bass tones coming across the line were a reminder that I hadn't made him up. What I could make out of his seductive tones, anyway! He had called me from his car because he had to run an errand in a town an hour out of Bozeman and the signal was damned spotty.

Not the most favorable condition in which to chat about romantic aspirations! He was distracted, too, and I hadn't anticipated that, either. That's not to say we didn't have a pleasant convo. We did! He told me more about his career and his kids and his political views. I found myself holding back somewhat since it was just hard to talk doing the Bluetooth shuffle. Oh, don't get me wrong, I participated in our chat for sure. I just ended up keeping things strictly platonic. He didn't open the door otherwise and I wasn't going to even touch the doorknob this time.

Yeah, this getting to know each other thing wasn't going the way I'd envisioned, at least not yet. You know how you can message or e-mail someone a whole paragraph and they reply with one-and-two-sentence replies that only touch on part of what you said? Keith was turning out to be one of those. Not me; I can bust out a pageful and still not say everything I want to. Again, words guy. So we were different in that way, which was okay – I just wasn't exactly sure what to do with it.

Then the weekend came where I didn't hear from Keith at all. I was supposed to; he said he would get in touch with me from the next comic con and we could set up our next phone call. Friday...Saturday...Sunday... nothing. Oh, I knew how busy he had to be between autographs and drawing pictures for fans and working on commissioned art once he got back to his hotel room – the way I had commissioned him to do my book cover. Plus he had to squeeze in time for his personal projects.

On an intellectual level, I was down with all of that.

Emotionally? Man, I agonized. Anxiety shot up in me like a puck hitting the bell on a high striker at a carnival. Try as I might, I couldn't reason myself out of it. *Breathe, Brody, breathe. There's no reason for this.* I spent the weekend going to the gym and taking drives and doing mindfulness stuff and basically just trying to talk my heart down off the ceiling. I did have enough presence of mind not to contact Keith myself that weekend. No, I was not going to come off as desperate by acting on the near-panic I was actually ashamed of, no matter how those feelings tried to generate impulses in me to ask why I hadn't heard from him or even just passive-aggressively write "Hey, how it's going out there?" I was at least proud of myself for that restraint.

Monday came, and still nothing. I was torn between everything I described and just gently being honest with him about how it felt not hearing from him when he said I would. I dashed off a quick note simply admitting I'd been disappointed by the silence. I didn't make a big deal out of it, but if something was going to develop between us down the road, I figured I shouldn't start by smothering my feelings. I pressed send and went to the gym again, trying to work off my frustration. While on the elliptical a notification flashed across my phone. It was Keith.

He apologized profusely – the con had been notably stressful, over and above his not being able to get on top of the commission work he had promised clients he'd get done. After it was over he'd stolen away to clear his head. What could I say to that? I was proud of him for taking care of himself, and told him so. Despite my own emotional hangover, I asked into the possibility of a second phone call, and we got our appointment apps to agree on a time.

We kept having to reschedule, but the call finally did happen...and so did that Bluetooth in the car again! Couldn't be helped – Keith was on his way to help his son with something on the outskirts of town. Hey, Keith could have flaked completely, so I was grateful he kept his promise to call despite the distraction. We ended up talking for forty-five minutes – our longest chat since the hotel.

I did take occasional notes. I wanted to remember his favorite bands and his children's names, things like that. Maybe one day those details might come in handy. I know what you're thinking – *Dude, you're looking at a long-distance thing at best. He lives hundreds of miles away.* I knew that. And of course it was far too early to be contemplating anything along those lines. But I gotta tell ya...I wasn't married to Reno and if things developed enough...well, I'd be happy to give U-Haul another call, let's leave it at that.

The chat was really nice, despite him driving through rural areas and the signal cutting out from time to time. For that reason I kept holding back on what I really wanted to talk about. Not that the getting-to-know-you stuff wasn't awesome. I could tell Keith was getting ready to wrap up and I was facing having to spend another week or two stuffing down my hopes until we could get on a more secure phone call; it was nothing that felt right getting into over text. So though I had a bowling ball in my stomach (thank you Tori Amos), I made myself go for it, the way I'd had to the fateful night all this started. Ah, to one day not always get so nervous. But it seems to be my metabolism.

I asked for one more moment before we hung up. I told Keith that I liked him – as much as you can like someone you don't know that well yet. I said that I realized making out in a hotel room can easily be a one-time thing, so I wanted to see if he might be on the same page in terms of there being a possibility something happening between us. Or at least the same chapter. Hell, the same book.

I breathed a little sigh of relief when Keith replied that he wouldn't have kissed me if he didn't like me, and that he did want us to keep learning about each other. He pointed out he couldn't be sure about anything yet, as we were still closer to strangers than anything else. But as far as he was concerned, the door was open, and he was still looking forward to our next get-together.

The reason it was only a little sigh was because I got thrown a curve ball, too. He told me he'd been dating a couple of guys in his area. I wish I could tell you that *didn't* throw me. Yet he was single and he'd met these dudes before me. People often date more than one person at a time. Well, most people, anyway. I knew I'd find it too confusing to go out with multiple men. This news did push some old buttons from my time in the open relationship – Keith's other guys were probably more in shape, more successful, more fun in bed...gah.

On the flip side, I reminded myself that if Keith were truly under the spell of either of these datemates, he wouldn't be interested in me. The poly thing might be a feature of most gay guys, but I could tell from our first meeting that Keith didn't play the field. If he did, I would never have started all this in the first place. Keith didn't seem serious about either of these fellows and he did say he had no plan or agenda about romance at the moment. He just wanted to see where things went. And now, from all indicators, I was included in that.

Only thing that really sucked is that my apparent rivals probably got to kiss Keith and likely more – and I was relegated to envisioning him in bed beside me when I went to sleep at night. This all just made the four weeks until our reunion feel that much further away. But you know what? I decided to try to shut up my always active brain with some glass-half-full mojo. A month ago...well, a month ago, none of this was an issue. Because there wasn't this chance at romance, peripheral as it might currently be. Okay, it was dusting off some old crap and insecurities and firing up needs I'd learned to bury the last few years. For all that, there was no denying that whatever this was with Keith was already a step in the right direction. And then there was that little twinkle I sensed from him toward the end of our phone call. I couldn't have imagined it. That was enough to carry me through at least the next several days.

3

WE TALKED AGAIN JUST over a week later. It was getting so we were, indeed, doing phoners once a week. I liked it! This chat wasn't romantic, either, but we did still get into a lot of subjects and beliefs, likes and dislikes, etc. Though part of me would have been okay with a dash of flirtation here and there, I figured maybe there was something to cementing a friendship first. That was a beat I always managed to miss with the guys in my past. It was either jump into an involvement and/or jump into bed, then I get the feels perhaps faster than is healthy, some would say. Really getting to know Keith first before any of that seemed like a good bit of cycle-breaking.

I was a little more nervous this conversation. Maybe because it would be the last one before we finally met up in Baltimore the following week. He sounded tired already – he'd warned me his would be a hectic summer, and having to be at cons virtually every weekend fulfilled that prophecy. I hoped I'd be able to provide a welcome diversion at this one and help him unwind a bit.

During the day, I could attend the con – he was getting me a pass – and surely I could ease some of his pressure by assisting at his booth. We could yap over lunch, but when the con was done for the day, we could go out for a much more leisurely dinner, spend some time alone together. As for picking up where we left off at the hotel in San Franscisco, which had been his original suggestion...oh, yes. I wanted to make sure the electricity that fired off between us wasn't just a fluke. And to see if the loving way he kissed extended to more carnal activities.

I also wanted to be as honest with him as we'd been since our initial social media messages. I wanted to tell him I was catching the beginnings of feelings for him. That I wanted us to go out on a real date. Both being in Baltimore for the con would make a first date doable, but I also had some ideas on how we could continue to date after that despite the sixteen-hour drive that separated us. It wouldn't be that difficult to visit each other for a couple of days here and there once fall kicked in and things slowed down for him as he predicted. I felt pretty good about all this. I wasn't going to ask him to marry me; I just thought it would be a plausible way for us to open up the romantic possibilities and get to know each other in that regard as well.

Finally, it was time for him to fly to Baltimore, and I Philly. It bothered me that we hadn't made definite plans for the big day – such as where to meet, what time, and all that. It hadn't been for lack of trying. I certainly had sent more than one trademark verbose, enthusiastic message. It was frustrating, but I was sure between all his prep and rushing to the airport, he just hadn't had a chance to get back to me. Not like I'd never been in that sitch myself.

The day of, I still hadn't gotten confirmation of anything, but it seemed appropriate to jump on the freeway and head to Baltimore. Yuck, I'd forgotten the slow-go-stop-and-go of big cities. The two-hour drive took well over four. The only good thing about sitting bumper-to-bumper was that I was finally able to message with Keith about the logistics. Yes, kiddies, I know – texting and driving is bad. Please do not attempt this at home.

Things seemed pretty chaotic over there, according to him. Aside from the usual flurry of fans and costumes, they hadn't situated him near a plug, and his phone was dying. Worse, someone had stolen the pass I was supposed to receive so I could get into this thing! Hey, I know con passes are like Willy Wonka golden tickets and cost hella coin, but you don't just boost a vendor's guest pass. A pox on this bastard for making seeing Keith more complicated!

In trying to keep things short to conserve his phone battery, we agreed I'd text him when I got to the convention center so he could at least meet me at the door. It wasn't that important that I actually got into the con, though I had been looking forward to seeing him in his element. The private time meant much more to me.

I finally made it, but I had failed to take into account the fact that thousands of people had descended on Baltimore for this mega-con, and that they had all gotten there before me. Parking garages nearby were either full or charging up the wazoo. Hey, I was doing all right for myself, but I wasn't a billionaire. So I toured around the city's many one-way streets, dusk approaching, trying to find a more sensible option. Finally I found an unattended lot that only wanted twenty bucks...over a mile away from the convention center. Which meant I'd have to walk about a half an hour each way. *Oh, what the hell, Brody,* I told myself. *You wanted to lose weight anyway, and at least you wore comfortable shoes.*

I could tell by the increasing number of costume-clad people I was passing that I was getting closer. It was pitch dark by the time I got to the looming auditorium. Did that matter? Keith was just inside those doors! Or those doors...or maybe it was those doors. Who am I kidding; the place was enormous. And I had no idea where to even start looking for the man. I texted him as promised. And then I waited.

And waited. And waited some more. Talk about being on the outside looking in. But I'd waited two months to see Keith again; a little while longer wasn't going to make much difference. This was his work and it's not like he could stop what he was doing with a line-up of thirsty fans just to message me. If his phone still even had any juice, that is.

Exciting and interesting as it was to watch the ever-evolving parade of superheroes and anthropomorphic manga characters and arch villains, a sinking feeling in my stomach threatened to get bigger. Unfortunately, that's my default, expecting something negative. I tried to counteract it by remembering how lucky I was to even have a chance with someone like Keith, but it was quite the internal battle.

Eventually, he messaged back that he was almost done but had to take a quick business meeting; he asked me to sit tight and warned me his phone battery was in the single digits. Sit tight I did, willingly – besides, at that point, what else was there to do? I was just going to have to chalk this up as part of the adventure.

An hour went by. Then two. No Keith. I didn't want to interrupt his business meeting, but this was getting ridiculous. I mean, it was getting close to 11:00. Though I knew his phone was probably dead, I left him a couple of messages anyway. This wasn't much of an adventure anymore. At this rate I couldn't get a hotel near the convention center because every one I called was full. And it wasn't like I could drive back to my friend's place in Philly, as I was getting too tired to do so.

I felt panicked and angry and sad as I watched people leaving the auditorium for the night. I hovered near several of the doors, hoping I might be able to spot Keith. Nothing. People boarded busses and those who had actually paid good money to sleep on the sidewalk for the night were settling in. I almost considered that option myself, but I certainly hadn't come prepared for something like that. Another attempted call to Keith went straight to voice mail, so I determined the best course of action was just to go back to the rental car. Worse came to worst, I could sleep in it, which I wasn't above doing. It was safer than driving two hours butt-hurt and exhausted.

You're an idiot, Brody, I whipped myself as I trudged the thirty-plus minutes back to the parking lot. How did I ever think this was going to work out? Maybe he was really just like so many of the flake-ass men I'd known before! Don't pelt me with unknowns. My mind will fill in the blanks. And not usually not with glitter and unicorns.

Feeling utterly defeated, I made a final, sure-to-be-vain call to Keith. And he answered! He had just gotten to his hotel! His phone had indeed completely died, and he had looked for me at the auditorium as well; finally, not seeing me anywhere and having an early morning tomorrow, he'd grabbed a cab back to his room. He felt really bad.

We had been looking for each other at the same time – imagine that! This would have been funny if I wasn't so dead tired. Worn down from physical and emotional exhaustion, I went balls-out and asked if I could bunk with him at his hotel. Not for ugly-bumping, believe me. No way I was in the mood for that! I just needed a place to crash and he understood how there were no more accommodations within a decent radius, so he gave me the address and it was all I could do to get there.

"We have to stop meeting like this," I joked as he opened his door to me. He looked half-dead. The con so far had been crazier than expected. We hugged and I thanked him for allowing a last-minute guest. There were two beds; I'd be lying if I said I wasn't hoping we'd sleep in one, but this wasn't the time, and I knew it. He had to get up before sunrise and work on some of that commissioned artwork I told you about. We sat on our opposing beds and talked a little about various and sundry before finally getting ready for sleep. It was so good to be near him again, to hear his voice coming out of his mouth instead of a phone speaker. This wasn't anything close to what I had in mind, but I wasn't unmindful that the night ended with us seeing each other after all.

I never sleep well in strange places as a rule, but here I was, six, seven feet away from the man I had fledgling feelings for and there wasn't a damn thing I could do about it except watch him sleep. He snored a little! So cute.

I must have finally dozed because morning came all too quickly. He had already been up working and was getting out of the shower. I drifted in and out some more before he lightly shook me awake; I forced myself out of bed as I had offered to drive him to the convention center, rather than make him take another taxi. Is it so wrong to show a guy you could be a good partner?

We went down for the continental breakfast and talked about who remembers what. I had slept two, maybe three hours and wasn't at my conversational best. Still, there was something bonding about us sitting there having gone through this experience together. I was getting an insider's look at his world and what he had to deal with working these cons. The time came for me to take him back to this one. With his fully-charged phone, but still no guest pass to allow me entrance, we made plans to meet for lunch. During which we would discuss the immediate future – after he was done here, as he had told me from the beginning, he was driving up to Philadelphia. He would see friends...work-related folks...and me.

Finally I would get to tell him what I'd been feeling! I contented myself with that and "dropped him off at work", again feeling like we had coupled up. He gave me a big hug before he got out of my rental and I made my way back to that mile-away parking lot to stash the car ahead of our lunch date. Didn't really want to drop another twenty dollars there, but damn it, this time it would be worth it.

I'd have to wait around again the whole morning. Oh well. I did the half-hour walk feeling much more energized despite the lack of sleep...until something happened I hadn't counted on. Con security had put up barricades; you couldn't go past a certain point without that coveted pass – the one I did not have in my possession. Why this wasn't a thing the night before, I didn't know, but once again, I wasn't going to be able to get anywhere near Keith. It was becoming like one of those rom-coms where the couple keeps missing each other and only gets together right before the end credits.

Keith and I did some humorous messaging about our plight. It really did seem some force was conspiring to keep us apart during this con, so we called it a wash and opted to try again in a couple of days on "my" turf. I decided that would be all right, even after all the hoops I'd just jumped through trying to see him. (It can't be said determination isn't one of my attributes.) At least once we were in the 215 and 267, he wouldn't be working, and there wouldn't be a comic con throwing up obstacles at every turn. So I wished him well and carefully drove the two hours successfully despite barely keeping my eyes open. Hope continued to spring eternal. We'd soon be together at long last; I would ask him to go out with me right then and there. Plus I'd never stopped looking forward to more of that huggin' and kissin'. Nothing was going to get in the way this time. I could feel it.

THE THIRD AND FINAL day of Keith's con arrived. Aside from alerting him that I'd gotten to my friends in Philly okay, I thought giving him some breathing room would be best. Perhaps the Baltimore con was an exception, but if they were all that huge and chaotic, no wonder he'd looked so frazzled. We'd see each other tomorrow, anyway. Hallelujah!

Besides, I had plenty to busy myself with. Remember, I was here for my own book event later in the week and there were preparations that had to be made. As Keith and I had both concurred, publishers only do so much. So the onus was on us. And I couldn't just use my friends' place as a hostel; I wanted to hang with them, too, and did.

I checked in with Keith the next morning. He had survived the con and cited it as the busiest one he'd ever worked in Baltimore. Now he was just waiting for his rental car; once obtained, he would make the drive up to the City of Brotherly Love.

The hours passed. Keith eventually wrote that he wasn't going to get access to his car until well after dinner. He was really frustrated. He'd have to scrap tonight and leave early tomorrow for Phoenix.

The hell? He was just gonna throw our baby

relationship out with the bath water and bolt because he couldn't get a rental car? I guess after stretching my patience out to the limit over the weekend, I had run out of it. Worse, I felt this whole chance at romance slipping through my fingers. I'm not gonna lie – I had a bit of a meltdown in the presence of my friends and hosts. Blessed be, they knew well my tendency toward heightened emotionality and were super supportive.

As I mentioned earlier, I'd done really well about not contacting Keith when I was all over the place. But here I slipped and it exposed more than one crack in my "I have it together" resolve. I guess, in retrospect, it wasn't that bad. I said I understood his frustration but I really didn't want him to go. I had been looking so forward to seeing him and there was so much I wanted to tell him – was he available for a call? I at least limited my message to that.

Somewhere between the burning in my face and fighting off the urge to cry, I came to a mortifying realization. Maybe he hadn't meant Phoenix, as in Arizona. Maybe he had meant Phoenix, as in the name of the publisher he draws for, who had a corporate office in Philadelphia and which he'd referenced before in our phone calls. God, could I have been that dumb?

I sent a brief inquiry about it and he laughed it off with an "LOL". Of course, Phoenix, his employer. I sat there relieved, but in total disbelief. If the ground could have opened up and swallowed me in that moment, I would have found that quite welcome. What an ass I'd made of myself. I had assumed the worst and gone into a tailspin and who knows what he thought of me now. Yes, we'd established from the beginning that we both had some depression/anxiety stuff we grappled with. That didn't mean I wanted him to see it. Not at this stage.

Try again tomorrow, that was my acquired philosophy. Sometimes you just have to give up on a day and start over the next. That tomorrow came and Keith let me know he had finally gotten into town. He was going to do his meetings and what-not. After that, we would firm up our own plans! What I was going to wear, what was I going to do with this curly hair that had a mind of its own, what I was going to say? I wasn't in love with him, no – I wouldn't let myself get to that point yet, which was an improvement over the way my heart used to operate – but I looked forward to telling him over a nice, dimly-lit dinner somewhere about my burgeoning feelings. I'd be content with holding hands and kissing. But if "the drought" were to end that night I would not say no. After the more-suspenseful-than-expected waiting I had done, the physical desire to be near him was becoming overwhelming.

There was no way I could prepare for what happened next. A couple of new lines appeared on my screen: his son had been in an accident and he had to fly home immediately. In fact, he was on his way to the airport as he texted me.

Of course he had to go home. What was I supposed to do, pull a "What about me?" We barely knew each other and his family had to come first. And even in some future that saw us together as a loving couple, I wouldn't think twice about being supportive of him in his time of need. I admired him for dropping everything for his kids. That last part I let him know as I said I understood and wished him and his son well.

That was the Zen part of me kicking in. The rest of me? Not so much.

It was like something had been ripped out of me. I was numb, yet everything seemed to ache at the same time. To say my disappointment was bitter was a masterpiece of understatement. But I have always believed the show must go on, and I had my own show to do, of sorts, with my book event 48 hours away. I made myself get back to work and it was even fortuitous that I had work to lose myself in, even if my stomach was in knots the rest of the day.

It didn't help that my hosts were going out of town and I'd agreed to dog sit. The whole day before my event I was alone except for the dog and the hours crawled by at a pace that would make a snail seem speedy. Forgive the melodrama, but it was a kind of torture to me.

My book event came, and I was able to throw myself into it. You may recall it was part of a three-day sci-fi conference, so I had a chance to observe and mingle and rise above the black hole of feelings that seemed determined to stay with me. Keith and I even did a little messaging in the middle of it all – his son was going to be okay and would be out of the hospital soon. He apologized for the crossed wires and missed opportunities. Maybe we could salvage this whole thing, I thought. With his son out of danger – I never would have suggested it otherwise – I proposed we get on another phone call sooner than later. I put out some dates and times. But, while he would tell me how things were going, he didn't directly respond to the telephonic invite. Make that invites.

I was learning that my patience was formidable, but not inexhaustible. I just wanted to get us back on track, at least in terms of getting to know each other.

So I took a calculated risk and put forth the idea that I might change my flight home and swing by Bozeman for a visit first. It wasn't that far off from what I'd had in mind overall. A few more days passed. Finally he replied there was too much going on; it had gotten so he didn't have time to spend with his family, and he was emotionally and physically drained. As you might have guessed, he nixed the visit. Maybe it was a little too radical to suggest given we were still more strangers than anything else. And maybe you're thinking, *You know, Brody, it sounds like the guy really wasn't that into you.*

The odds were always more that it wouldn't work out than it would. However, I didn't see any reason to cut and run yet. There was still a chance; the timing was just all off right now. I wouldn't push my friends if they were clearly telling me they were stressed. Keith regretted being distant and offered to chat soon.

Was I making myself too available, being too pliable, letting him control the narrative? Possibly. Certainly I was aware of my history having done all those things, especially in that open relationship I mentioned. But I knew how busy Keith was. I guess I was still banking on his repeated contentions that things would calm down once summer was over. I'd just have to stick it out until fall came and see where we were then.

I backed off except for small talk – his son was home and recovering nicely. Did I say I backed off? I did squeeze in a request for a do-over phone call here and there. He was on board and told me he'd have some time the following week after this latest in a barrage of cons. Too bad that aside from our usual messaging which was comprised of longer paragraphs from me and few-liners from him, "talk soon" and "let's chat tomorrow" and "let's chat this weekend" ended up being more of the same. His intentions were good; they had to be. It's just that by now it had been a month since the Baltimore debacle, and I was no closer to actually having a phone-to-phone conversation with him than I was when I dropped him off in front of the convention center that morning.

I couldn't stand it anymore. Day after day I was having to stuff down my hopes and pretend they didn't matter. They did matter. *Express yourself, don't repress yourself,* as the wise woman said. So I started drafting an e-mail to him, not that we did much communicating through that medium. It was just going to be longer than a typical social media message and I didn't want it to be part of that scroll for all eternity. Or at least until one of us deleted it.

I screwed up my courage and hit send after a few rewrites. Then I sent him a quick text to expect it. Owing to how hard it had become to get replies from him with the seemingly constant whirlwind going on around him, I "joked" for him not to take too long getting back to me – cliffhangers were only fun on TV.

5

WHAT WAS THAT I was saying about cliffhangers? Days went by, and no acknowledgement of what I had written in my e-mail missive. In a nutshell, I told Keith what I told you about wanting to go out on a proper date, seeing if San Francisco had been a fluke. I admitted I'd been thinking we might be good for each other. And yes, that I had some embryonic feelings for him, though I realized I didn't know him well enough yet to let myself go there.

I just wanted for us to keep getting to know each other, except on a deeper level. I figured that was the only way to find out what green lights or deal-breakers there might be in terms of going past friendship. I also recalled what he'd said about not having a plan or an agenda – I agreed that no romantic connection should be forced, but you don't plant a seed and then throw up your hands as to whether it grows. You water it, nurture it. If it comes up or not is out of our control. Same endgame, just different ways of arriving at it. And I still thought he was adorable.

That wasn't so bad, right? It's not like I was screaming "Keith love me nowwwwwww", or even like that could be read between the lines. Reasonably healthy, I thought. You're certainly free to think otherwise.

As to what Keith thought, the waiting game began anew. After a few days, I made casual mention of the e-mail I'd sent and he replied with, "You sent me an e-mail?" Turned out it had made its way into his junk folder. Stupid algorithms. Then again, it's not like we e-mailed regularly enough for his inbox to recognize me; our chats had been restricted to social media messaging and the occasional text.

Finally he said that he'd read my "thoughtful" e-mail (wasn't exactly sure how to take that word) and that he'd respond but it would have to be from the next city he was travelling to that weekend. Hopeful as I was, I kind of wondered how he'd squeeze that in between all his other con duties, now having witnessed them...and I wasn't wrong. The weekend came and went and there was no notification with his name on it.

You can lead a horse to water, but you can't make him e-mail back. What could I do? I couldn't keep haranguing him with constant reminders. He knew what was on my mind. But I have to admit, this was getting more than a little ridiculous. I waited at least a week – I don't remember now how long it was – and during that time I realized I'd spent a good chunk dancing to his tune, while we hadn't even cued up mine.

I tried to view it as an exercise in finding that balance in a relationship where you're mindful of your partner's needs while not forgetting about your own. I went ahead and wrote him that I understood how overwhelmed he was, that I wanted to be sensitive to that and not add to it...yet I had to be sensitive to myself as well. It had already been three weeks since my e-mail – if time for a proper written response was lacking, how about just bottom-lining it and letting me know if he wanted us to keep getting to know each other or not? Or we could just cover it on the phone in a few minutes. I also admitted I was frustrated. I hadn't come this far to clam up about my feelings.

He sighed that things always seemed to come up... work stuff, family stuff. It had gotten out of hand. He did acknowledge one specific point in my message by admitting, "I'm frustrating, I know."

For real, you just noticed?

I told you my patience wasn't inexhaustible. I tried to keep myself busy as days added up to a week and then that week added up to two. I began to face the possibility that things with Keith were just dead in the water, beyond repair.

Out of the blue he writes that he hasn't forgotten about me, and engages me in a little how-are-you-doing chatter. What the hell, I'd bite. Friendly banter is still communication. Even when it trickles over several days. I wasn't going to give him any more than he was giving me; I matched his one-liners with one-liners. And then matched it with nothing at all, once again.

As much as I didn't want to admit it, it increasingly seemed like I'd already gotten my answer to my e-mail, and without a key being stroked. Maybe it was time to find a towel and throw it in. Yet, despite what logic might dictate, I wasn't ready to give up. I'd try it one more time.

In this note I was a little firmer than I had been. Was he that busy? Did he just not want to hurt my feelings with his answer? How would *he* feel if he'd opened up to me and then I went that long without addressing it? Had I scared him off? I knew I was a hot mess on the best of days. But I was still well worth getting to know and if I thought he wasn't I wouldn't still be bothering.

He didn't blame me, he said. He'd been avoiding everyone and was so far behind on things he was only now paying bills from a couple of months ago. But as he was finally able to see the light at the end of the tunnel between his son being fully recovered and the comic con season dying down, he promised me an answer the coming weekend. "Promise" in capital letters. PROMISE.

Every time he wrote back about how thinly stretched he was, I felt bad and started to wonder if I was being too pushy. I certainly didn't expect to be a priority. It's not like we were involved in any kind of way. But damn, boy. Chances at romance didn't just come along every day.

So much for capital letter promises. Said weekend came and went with no word. Monday, however, was a different story.

6

I SAW HIS MESSAGE on my phone as I was waking up and didn't even get out of bed to read it. Part of me was very hesitant, but if it was good news, I guessed I should hear it that much faster, and if it was bad news, then getting right to it would be like ripping off a Band-Aid.

Keith thanked me for having the patience of a saint. He liked me, and said several times how nice I was. He enjoyed meeting me, and when he kissed me, he meant it. When he chose to get to know me better, he meant it. He just wasn't feeling me romantically. Said he'd know by now if there were any fireworks.

If it was possible to experience relief and agony at the same time, I was. I mean, at least I wouldn't have to wait for his responses anymore, which had become maddening. But whatever hope I had held onto the past few months...now I had no reason left to hold on to it.

He went on to say he was surprised no one had snatched me up yet; I had looks and personality and he hoped we could continue on as friends. He then got super real and confessed that with his schedule, dating would be next to impossible even if he thought we had that kind of potential. He didn't like that he ended up putting everyone in his life on the backburner because of his work. In fact, he wasn't looking for a romantic relationship at all. Not after his long marriage and the couple of relationships he'd had with men afterwards, which apparently had been intense enough that he now just wanted to take a break from all that and spend more time with his family.

He finished by saying he cared about me and hoped he hadn't led me on. Thanking me for my kindness, he added that he wanted to keep chatting with me.

And that was that.

Cue up Juice Newton's *Break It to Me Gently.*

That was the bitch of the whole thing. I don't think I had ever had it broken to me so gently. *He* was kind, up until the very end.

I tried to go on with my day as usual. I went to the gym and my training group. But when we got to the kickboxing section, I did boot the trainer's guard pads harder than I normally would have.

I spent the next several days in sort of a calm tailspin. I appreciated how gentle he was closing the romantic door. I could understand how he'd not be in the market for a relationship. And yet it as was hard to erase the growing feelings I still had for him as it was the frustration and anxiety I had felt all those weeks not being able to connect with him. I even started to entertain the thoughts of the hypnotherapist I had been seeing, who suggested Keith had avoided me on purpose during the Baltimore con and made up his son's emergency to get out of seeing me. Not that I entertained it long. And Ms. Hypnotherapist did not receive another visit from me after that.

But the one thing she had taught me was the

importance of having an open heart. Sounds simple, and I thought my heart had been open for years, to an extreme, even. Our initial session taught me that mine wasn't as ready to receive as I'd thought. So I'd put some work into fixing that – and then I met Keith. It was like the perfect manifestation of this new way of existing I was pursuing.

It was tempting to just point my finger at Keith, but what is it they say? When you point the finger, you have three fingers pointing back at you. Had I gone into this afraid it was going to tank from the start? Did I act from that place, especially in those times when I hadn't heard from him as quickly as I wanted to? I had to answer with a qualified yes, but I wouldn't have been fair to myself if I hadn't added that I was aware of my thoughts and behavior and honestly had taken actions to change them during my whole experience with Keith. And part of that now was, I wasn't going to respond to Keith's friend-zoning from any kind of impulse. It would have to wait.

If he had been a dick, I wouldn't have bothered. It was because he had been so kind that I felt acknowledgement of his words was only right. Besides, at this point, I had nothing left to lose!

After two weeks passed, I sat down and told him it wasn't like I hadn't seen his cold water coming – I was disappointed and it hurt. I hadn't fallen in love with him... but it wouldn't have been much of a fall. For what it was worth, all I'd been asking was to resume getting to know each other with an eye toward a date. And here I'd waited through the summer to get to a less time-consuming autumn for him, only to have autumn bring the fall.

I divulged that part of me wanted to try to change his mind, because it was like he closed the door on any chance to find out how compatible we might have been before it could reach the front porch. I wasn't going to do that, but what I didn't really understand was his saying he wasn't looking for an involvement. Because that wasn't the impression I'd gotten from our phone calls, and certainly if I had thought that when we first met, I wouldn't have set these wheels in motion. Maybe he'd only recently realized he wasn't available. Maybe my persistence had helped him realize it.

While I accepted his overture of friendship, I did mention it would have to happen somewhere down the line. I needed a little time, and I would let him initiate it. Also – and I concede some of my anger flashed through on this one – my word to the wise was, next time someone laid out their heart to him, not to wait seven weeks to reply one way or the other. His having done that had made things much more difficult, and had been bad form.

There. I got a zinger in there, didn't I. Even if it was the truth.

There was more, and in retrospect I shouldn't have been so verbose, but like I told you, that's how I roll. Oh. I did "blurt" out that from knowing other workaholics in my life (including myself), keeping yourself that busy is usually a sign of running from something. Maybe I shouldn't have gone there. But then, you don't have to take any emotional chances when you bury yourself in work. Just sayin'.

I thanked him for caring about me. Better to have

liked and lost and all that. Of course I read my missive over several times. Then I clicked.

For the first time since before we'd met in person, I hadn't written expecting an answer. Amazingly, several days later, I got one. He hated hurting me. He valued the fact that we'd connected and had so much in common. He just was coming to believe even more strongly that he didn't want anything more than friendship with anyone, period. He couldn't even reply to e-mails promptly. He wasn't boyfriend material.

He apologized again for letting me down and repeated his desire for us to remain a part of each other's lives. I did want that. I've found it's hard enough to even find friends that get me, who I can be my emotional, quirky self around. You don't just turn a friend like that away.

So, we agreed to be friends.

And then...nothing.

7

MAYBE IT WAS JUST as well. I did need time to "get over" Keith, as much as you can get over someone you say you weren't in love with. Another potential benefit to no contact with him was that it would give me time to put the sleeping giant back into hibernation. I didn't relish the idea of "the drought" continuing in earnest, especially after the emotional and sexual components of me had been reawakened these past months. But it was going to have to be.

Soon the calendar was down to one page. I was going to have to contact him on a year-end business matter regarding the artwork he'd done for me. Talking shop was probably safer than anything else at this point, but I admit I hesitated messaging him. It was all right. In fact, he was downright talkative by comparison as we worked out details and got into what the other was doing for Christmas. Kinda made me feel good, being in regular contact again for a few days.

Was he still down for friendship in the new year? I wanted to know. Yes, he was on board. We got a few weeks into January with no communication, so I sent one catchy line and a cute GIF to try and get that ball rolling. He got back to me in a few hours and said he was trying to find more balance in his schedule for the coming year. The friend in me replied I thought that was a much healthier way to approach things than the way he had run himself ragged over the summer. The romantic in me silently hoped maybe that meant there'd be time for... *Oh, Brody, knock it off.*

Took a week for him to respond to that, after which I went daredevil. See, Carson City, half an hour or so south of me, was having its very first comic con. I was going to give it a shot, and I suggested he might like to do the same. He wouldn't even have to spring for a hotel like usual (tax write-offs though they may be). He'd be more than welcome to crash on my couch. What did he think?

All right, fine, yeah. I did have ulterior motives. I mean, if that just ended up being a friendship interaction, at least we'd get to hang out and actually have conversations in person. Or...okay, you know where this is going. Maybe being near each other again, we could rediscover that spark that went off like a supernova but now barely flickered like a star several light years away.

He never replied to the invite. At all. Like, months-went-by-never.

Perhaps he had been perceptive enough to sense my opportunistic altruism in trying to use the con to have him over as my houseguest, and thought *Clearly this guy isn't getting the message.* Ah, maybe I was foolish to try. It just had seemed so perfect, having a con so nearby. A con I ended up working myself, a con I was underwhelmed by. Carson City wasn't really into my book. And in trying to start something romantic with Keith, I had turned that very book which I'd been really passionate about into something painful by virtue of his cover art.

Some friendship *this* was turning out to be.

8

LIFE WENT ON. SOME days I didn't think of Keith at all and other days I still felt that sting of disappointment. *Jesus Christ,* I know you're all thinking. *Enough about your feelings, already. Fixating, much, Brody?* Yes, I see the carpet you're calling me on. Here was a guy I'd shared one kiss with, met twice, had a handful of phone calls with. And I still couldn't get him off my mind. Maybe it was because I knew there weren't many guys I was going to find going forward that ticked as many of my boxes as Keith had.

I'm also fully willing to admit that perhaps I had developed feelings for the fantasy of Keith, the idea of him, rather than the real person. I'd certainly had enough time to build him up into something unrealistic, and the silences and constant missed opportunities had created a lot of gaps I could fill in with whatever I wanted. Look, I know my character defects and it wasn't the first time I'd pulled that on myself. And I'm not gonna lie – I liked liking someone again. I liked there being a possibility of someone to love again. That's what made me hang in there when I probably should have bailed on the guy. And that's what was making it so hard to let go of him now. Who the hell wants to go back to warping through empty space after finally finding a potentially life-sustaining planet?

Keith dropped me a standard birthday greeting on social media when that day came. I sent him a personal, trademark quirky but much-pithier-than-usual message on the occasion of his own birth. That was really it. I was not going to initiate any further contact with him. It wasn't so much from a "So there!" standpoint. He knew how to get in touch. If he wanted to communicate with me, he could make the first damn move.

I suppose it would have been very easy to just find someone new and forget about him. Easy as it is to find someone new who doesn't just want to fuck around. Truthfully, I wasn't ready. I had been the Rebound King in my earlier days and I had eventually learned the value of waiting until I was truly emotionally available before rushing headlong into another involvement. Having done so hadn't been fair to me, but more than that, it hadn't been fair to the new guys. Rebounds are a disaster waiting to happen. For me, anyway. So I was going to have to ride this out, however long it took.

It didn't work out between Keith and me and it was as simple as that. I felt one thing, he felt another; it happens. I genuinely did wish him well. Though I did need reminders from time to time. I found one in a book I read – a passage that encouraged me to wish him happiness, safety, strength and ease. Done. Many times, over and over. I honestly hoped he was okay, healthy, that he was lessening the craziness in his life and getting to see his kids more regularly.

Some days I turned the microscope on myself. What had I done wrong? How could I have approached things differently? Would the outcome had been the same if I'd come less from a place of fear and more from a place of self-assurance? What about all this heart-opening stuff the hypnotherapist had told me about? Sometimes during my brief interaction with Keith I'd felt I'd achieved it, like I could sense the energy of the universe flowing through me. More familiar, though, was that old tightness in my chest, like my heart was most definitely cut off from that energy. Madonna was right. You *are* frozen when your heart's not open.

Other days, often out of nowhere, I'd feel angry. I'd see his artwork on a publication or hear his favorite band in a store and think *What a bastard.* It wasn't that he realized he didn't want a relationship after hinting he did, or that he decided he didn't see me filling that role in his life. It was that he'd made all this noise about being friends, and been so damn nice about it – and then had zero follow-through. It was like I didn't even exist to him. That hurt. Hence the anger. Because isn't anger just hurt turned inward?

I got my work done. I hung out with friends and stopped mentioning Keith's name to them. I took care of family obligations and ran my household. In truth, I was tired of thinking about him and very much wanted to be clear of feelings of any description having to do with him. Despite not being able to will them away, the best I could do was acknowledge them and keep going. At times I thought it would be a lot easier to move past all this if Keith and I had had some actual closure, a real conversation that would help me feel complete about things. There was the occasional temptation to contact him and ask for it. But I wasn't going to. If he was going to ghost me, I was going to ghost him. And so there was no closure to be had, outside of whatever peace I could come to on my own.

In this midst of these psychological peaks and valleys, someone told me about a small comic con happening in Redding, California that was only a three-and-a-half-hour drive from me. It wasn't one of the better-known events, but I decided I would work it to perhaps reach a different subset of potential customers – and because, if you must know, I thought the trip and the change in environment would go a long way toward shaking up my existence and clearing out the cobwebs.

Wasn't I afraid I would run into Keith? Hell, no. Due to the popularity and high profile of Keith's publisher, there was no way he'd be at such a comparatively tiny con. I was cleared for take-off. I even made up my mind I was going to have fun at this thing.

Son of a bitch if he didn't end up having a table kitty-corner from mine, giving us a clear damn view of each other.

9

WELL, CLEARLY, I HADN'T thought to check the vendor list to see who else was going to be there. And again, there hadn't really been any reason to. Whatever my emotional upheaval about him, he was still an incredible artist – incredible enough I'd have thought a smaller event like this was beneath him.

Called that one, didn't I!

I honestly thought about bailing, but I'd already set up. More importantly, I'd already spent the money on the space and the trip. Plus blabbed enough on social media that I was going to be there.

It occurred to me I could try and switch tables. No, scratch that. No sense in inconveniencing the organizers or another vendor, and as soon as I started relocating my stuff Keith would know I was running away from him. I wasn't going to give him that satisfaction, cliché as that sounded.

And then I became aware of another fresh layer of horror.

It was his artwork on my blasted cover. Ultimately our mutual fans were going to make the connection and want to talk to us together, get autographs, the works. Why wasn't there a trap door under this table I could escape through? Could I offer one of these guys money for his Iron Man helmet and plop it on my head when Keith wasn't looking so I could walk out undetected?

Crap. Well, this buttercup was going to have to suck it up. I was here to work. If I had to interact with him, it was going to be business and nothing but. But only assuming that became necessary. In the meantime, I formulated a plan of avoidance in plain sight I hoped would make James Bond proud. (The Daniel Craig version, thank you very much. Oh, baby.) If Keith could put a wall in place after being all kumbaya about a post-flirtation friendship, I was going to make his look like a wet piece of cardboard. Treat *me* like shit and then act like nothing happened. No, ma'am. You tried it. You motherfucking tried it.

I didn't look in his direction outside of the occasional peripheral glance; fortunately, he proved popular enough that he didn't have many chances to stop by my table. Our eyes did meet once by accident when he had a free moment; he waved generously. I took that moment to straighten books that didn't need straightening. My work wasn't nearly as much in demand as his, but that was okay; I did move some product and managed to extend conversations with customers and the curious, even those who filled my ear with inconsequential, Captain Obvious word salad. Ordinarily that kind of repartée would have tested my patience. Now I welcomed it.

This is how the first couple of hours went. But with every ticking nanosecond I was aware that someone would eventually want a photo op with us or some kind of unofficial interview. I calmed myself with a false sense of security through that morning, as no one seemed ready to take advantage of our being in the same room. A few patrons and passersby asked about Keith's work, and I happily and genuinely pointed them in the direction of his table with no repercussions. Maybe I'd be able to get through the weekend without –

Nope. When a particularly enthusiastic visitor noticed Keith's signature style he absolutely had to get a picture with both of us. Right now! Mr. Man ran over to Keith, who, despite looking harried already, obligingly stepped away from his table and came over to mine. I'd done my share of acting in my time, and now it was time to give one helluva performance.

It wasn't easy. The hotel's banquet hall, possibly the entire universe, felt like it narrowed down to these few feet between me, him, and our oblivious fan. I gritted my teeth through selfies. I don't think it showed, but all the hurt, regret, and disillusionment cascaded through me at lightning speed. And the anger. I had to stay angry. It was the only way to keep above the wave of feelings and urges having Keith's beautiful bearded face near me in person again was generating. He smelled so good. I wanted him so bad. And I hated myself for it. For his part, Keith didn't seem particularly fazed one way or the other.

I thought that might be the end of it. But somehow Keith being away from his table and in an actual aisle with a fan attracted even more of them. The next little while became a complete blur. Let's face it – Keith's presence created greater interest in my lesser-known work, so I was signing and transacting up a storm. We took more selfies with people, I was as friendly as ever, and the whole time I sang the praises of Keith's talent. That part wasn't for show. I knew I'd been lucky to have his work emblazoned on my cover. I wasn't going to be so petty as to diss on him professionally because he hadn't done what my heart had wanted him to.

I didn't say much to him. Thankfully, I didn't have to. He ran back to his own table at times and I reveled in the relief that came with it. I took an extra long lunch, hoping I wouldn't run into him at whatever fast food joint I chose. It was tempting not to go back to the banquet hall, but my whole stash was there. As the afternoon wore on, there were a few more moments where fans wanted face time with both of us together. So I smiled and chatted and tried as hard as I could to keep engaged with people so I wouldn't end up alone with Keith. In fact, I probably screwed myself out of sales by closing up for the day early while he was busy with another cluster of cosplay conventioneers. I hoped to hell he wasn't also staying at this hotel, but, just in case, I ordered pizza, opened and closed the door like a spy, then shut myself in for the rest of the evening, praying he wouldn't ask the front desk if I was a guest.

He didn't. But my night's sleep wasn't the best. Several times I entertained the thought of going to the banquet hall and packing my *accoutrements* into the car and getting the hell outta Dodge. But they'd locked it up for the night. Damn trying to keep our junk from getting stolen anyway. I didn't know how I was going to get through a whole 'nother day of this. What if I just sat Keith down and told him what I was feeling?

Naw, fuck that. I had already stripped myself naked in front of him, emotionally speaking, several times and it hadn't gotten me anywhere. The fact that I hadn't heard from him for months despite his pledging friendship showed he wasn't interested in even that. The best thing I could do, I thought to myself as I paced the hotel room floor with only the bathroom light tunneling a path through its darkness, was stick to business. Barrel through, be polite, and make my escape gracefully.

Plus pull a *Star Trek* and employ evasive maneuvers. I made sure to show up good and late, long after he'd gotten there, and glory be, he was once again up to his eyeballs in admirers. I enjoyed a slower trickle, even if my bank wasn't. At one point our mutual attendance required more photos and interviews; he wished me good morning as he approached and I replied with a smiling grunt, quickly turning my attention to the task at hand. I'm kind of ashamed to admit I found repeated performances of our elbow-rubbing almost fun. I had to remind myself I was not there to have fun. At least not where Keith was concerned.

I again escaped for a long lunch – I got smart this time and hauled to-go burgers and fries up to my room, looking over my shoulder every step. I must have looked ridiculous coming back into the lobby with my eyes darting around; I actually stiffened myself against the hall's doorway and peered down the aisle to make sure Keith was at his table and engaged before I made a beeline for my own booth for the last few hours of this hell ride.

But that's weird, Brody, you're thinking. No, the weird part came not long after I sat down.

A bunch of costumed millennials I hadn't seen the previous day strolled by my table, not making eye contact with me. Okay, my stuff isn't your scene, whatever. Then one girl instantly recognized Keith's handiwork on my cover and tripped out. Seriously, this chick gushed so much over it I thought I was going to have to call the janitor. But when her friend pointed out that the artist was just across the way, she lost all control. It wasn't that she wanted a selfie with both of us like the other patrons. She wanted a picture with just him and my book. She practically grabbed a copy off my display to take over to him until I politely reminded her she'd have to pay for it first.

Her solution was to bulldoze her way ahead of the nice couple Keith was speaking to and about yank him out of his chair. After she brought him back to my table, she grudgingly plunked down the cash for my book, then proceeded to act like I was invisible. Some people are like that, especially in the fan world. I could have lived with that. But she was making such a ruckus over Keith that it got her friends all vocal, too, and they attracted a crowd that completely blocked my booth. Like anyone walking by couldn't even see me. A few of his admirers bought my merch yet also ran to him and acted like I didn't exist. I think Keith must have been in the middle of them but it was hard to tell; like locusts, the prattling, annoying swarm made their way back to his table, and from there I was just sitting there twiddling my thumbs.

I'd had enough.

With still another two hours of the con to go, I started dismantling my display and thrusting books into boxes. I wondered if I could pack up fast enough to get out of there before Keith could even notice I was gone. Maybe I owed Fangirl of the Century a debt of gratitude. She was *still* at the head of the crowd and Keith was signing things furiously. If I was lucky, I might be able to grab one of the hotel's luggage carts while no one had need of them and make the drive home tonight instead of tomorrow. I'd eat the damn money I spent on the hotel room. I didn't care.

Because I was exhausted between the lack of sleep, trying to recover from yesterday, and this bullshit today, I was running on pure adrenaline. And fury, which was giving me enough energy to finish packing the boxes and strip the table of any identifying decorations. I half stomped to the lobby and was indeed able to secure the vaunted luggage cart, hoping the desk clerk I'd asked for it wouldn't notice my resting scowl face.

I purposely kept my back to Keith and his swamped table as I stacked my boxes and paraphernalia on the cart. I was so immersed in my duty I didn't even notice the din dying down. The satisfied throng moving on.

Or Keith approaching me from behind.

"Leaving already?" came the voice I hadn't heard since I dropped him off at that crossed-wire Baltimore con all those months ago.

I didn't turn to look at him. "How terribly clever of you to figure that out."

Even without seeing him, I could tell my tone had thrown him off. "Hey, I'm sorry about what happened back there with those people and all. I feel bad, the way they were ignoring you."

"Oh, that's okay; I'm used to being ignored," I spat.

See, a funny thing happens when I'm overly tired, overly angry, overly depressed – or some combination of the above. I lose my impulse control. I once had a therapist tell me he'd rarely seen someone with such possession of that particular trait; it's kept me out of arguments and beds and free from STDs and just generally making choices that would otherwise put me in funky situations.

But without that impulse control, I start doing and saying things I would never ordinarily do. Like now.

"Look, I know you're upset," he was still forced to say to my back. "I didn't mean to take the focus off you. I sure as hell would be annoyed if the situation were reversed."

I stood up straight, but craned my head a bit in his direction. My eyes were flashing. "I don't care about that." I honestly meant it. "You're the celebrity in these circles, not me. If I hadn't thought your art worthy of that celebrity I wouldn't have approached you about working together in the first place." I went back to my box stacking.

"Then what's been eating you this entire con?" Keith wanted to know. "You've barely said two words to me. I thought we were going to be friends."

I turned around aghast, in slow-motion as I'd seen many times on soaps. This moment certainly merited it.

"Are you freakin' kidding me right now? You're gonna talk to *me* about friendship? You, Casper the Friendly Ghost?"

"What?"

"Don't 'what' me," I fumed. "You're the one who disappeared off the face of the earth after all this 'let's keep chatting' crap. I can't believe I fell for that. Oh, you care about me. Yeah, it really shows."

"I do care about you."

"Save it! Save it for the other guys you blow off. I don't wanna hear it."

Keith threw up his arms. "I get it. You're still hurt that I didn't want to pursue a relationship with you. I said I was sorry; I just haven't been in the market for – "

"You know what really hurts?" I looked him right in his eyes, those hazel beautiful eyes I would rather have gotten lost in than shot daggers at. "It's not like I was proposing. Yeah, maybe I fantasized about that shit, but all I was trying to do was get us back on track to getting to know each other again and go from there. There was so much I still wanted to know about you. Favorite color, favorite number, greatest fear – stuff like that. What you like to eat, childhood stuff. Your middle fucking name. You don't see me as boyfriend material – that happens. But we're not friends. We're acquaintances. Barely." I lifted a book out of an open box. "This is all we have in common. And that's not what I thought when we first met."

Keith's face was hard to read as I chucked the book back in the box. "I told you I barely see friends or family because of my schedule – "

"Dude, it's like Maya Angelou said: 'When someone shows you who they are, believe them the first time.' You're a flake, is what you are. You were when I almost had to bludgeon the finished cover out of you to make my deadline, you were when I came to meet you that day and you made me wait for hours. Some even say you flaked out on me in Baltimore on purpose – whatever! I do know that you completely flaked on this friendship you said you wanted, and if that's all you got, you can keep it. Even with a friend I deserve someone who participates as much as I do. And that someone sure as hell ain't you."

I didn't wait for a reaction. I rolled the luggage cart out of the hall, open box and all, with all the energy I could muster. I still had stuff by the table; I didn't give a shit. In the lobby I explained to one of the con organizers I'd have to come back later to get the rest of it – I made up some BS about having to visit a family member and I got the okay to come back while the hotel staff was cleaning up the room. Which is exactly what I did. Then I drove home a nervous bloody wreck. I probably shouldn't have gone off on Keith like that. But it was like they sang in that musical: he had it comin'. He had it comin'. He only had himself to blame.

10

ONCE THE SUN WAS up and I'd actually gotten some sleep and my impulse control was fully functional again, it was hard to believe the Redding comic con had even happened. Let alone ripping Keith a new asshole. I was really torn. On the one hand, I felt bad about having done it. It wasn't like me. And whatever chance may still have existed for a friendship was surely out the window now. On the other, I reminded myself there hadn't been a friendship anyway, so I really hadn't lost anything. And, as horrified as I was by my behavior, I also couldn't help being proud of myself. I had kept all that in for the better part of a year and it was good to have it out. I'd stood up for myself with him after, by his own admission, having been the very model of patience.

And I hadn't been wrong. I *did* deserve more and better, from all manner of relationships. I'd spent twelve years giving my ex the green light to sleep around on me even though it wasn't what I wanted. Hadn't I deserved better than that? I'd put up with Keith's silences and growing resistance and leaving my heart hanging out to dry for nearly two months while I waited for him to reject me. Didn't I deserve better than that?

You're damn right I did. And maybe it was time I tried being a better friend to the friends I did have. My self-absorption was legendary and I myself often got wrapped up in projects and deadlines and promotion to the detriment of relationships with people who actually cared about me. Like they say: if you're getting pissed off about the way someone's behaving, you have to take a look and see where you're behaving the same way. So I was looking.

The late morning sky was clear and so was a part of me, having let Keith know what time it was. At least now there wouldn't be any more of that angst about never hearing from him, about our post-could-have-been-romantic friendship dying on the vine. I'd poisoned the rest of the vineyard and it was time to plant seeds somewhere else.

And that I did. I had more writing to do, and more pushing the writing I'd already done. Behind Keith's cover image was one of the coolest stories I'd ever transmitted out of my fingers and a wider readership needed to know about it. I busied myself with sending cover letters and press releases and author copies to reviewers and podcasts and industry dignitaries and bookstores. For someone who hates rejection as much as I do, this can often be an exercise in frustration, putting yourself out there only to receive a small percentage of positive response.

So when you do manage to get a fish on your hook, that fish is golden. One of the bigger chain book establishments I'd been coveting put me on their event calendar in their Boise location for the following month. Which meant more press releases, tweets, e-mails and yes, even faxes to let people know this thing was happening. But that didn't matter. This was a coup and I was going to take full advantage of it. Not to mention express full gratitude to the universe for this coming into being.

Somewhere in the middle of all this activity, I caught myself. I'd been channelling Keith, hadn't I? Putting work over time with friends, time for me, and all that. So I took a gentle detour at the border of hypocrite territory and sent messages to my peeps, made a phone call or two. And there was the matter of that heart opening stuff I had given up on after I ended up in Keith's non-friend friend zone. I had closed back up, and that wasn't going to do me any good down the line, not romantically or professionally. Going forward I made a concerted effort to sit down once in a while, breathe into my heart, meditate on what it opening could and did feel like. A few minutes here and there, anyway.

On that score, I even crafted a personal ad to post on a dating app. You'll notice I didn't actually post the ad. I didn't want the box that would open to be Pandora's. Plus I hate that you have to register and post first before you can look at anyone else's profile. I know it's only fair that way. It's just I like to have the advantage. So sue me.

The day of the Boise event came. It was literally a lighter affair, as the bookstore had its own video equipment and I likewise didn't have to haul boxes of books with me the whole six-plus-hour drive, because the store was providing them. That also meant I'd have to work harder to sell more of them, but I felt good about this one. I had done up a fun little video presentation to tie in with my story and I could be rather gregarious in the spotlight considering how anxiety-filled I could be. And yes, Keith would be there in that his personifications of my characters stared at me from every copy. That was okay. As always, I would dutifully give him credit and point people to his web site. Maybe this time it wouldn't even sting doing it, not after clearing the smog out of my heart by yelling at him and doing the meditation stuff.

And you know what? It *did* go well! I'd expected a corporate bookstore to be all...well, corporate, especially compared to their independent counterparts. But these guys were super chill and enthusiastic, and so were the attendees. My video accompaniment was a hit and the audience asked intelligent and interesting questions – which believe me, wasn't always the case. It was symbiosis at its best; they were fired up, which got me fired up, which kept them fired up, and so on. In fact, I couldn't remember the last time an event had gone so well. Financially, too. These guys snatched up so many copies the store damn near ran out of them, and my hand damn near fell off from all the autographs (I never just write "best wishes"). It was glorious.

There was only one strange part about it. I find it's not good to isolate yourself when working events. So I try to make eye contact with folks so they'll feel included. I look over faces. Linger an extra second over the ones belonging to cute guys.

But there was this one dude in the back. There was something off about him. This dark straggly beard covered his face and it had an odd sheen. And don't get me wrong – fans of my type of work often consist of oddballs; it comes with the territory and you learn to embrace them. Except this guy made me nervous. He barely reacted to anything, and like I said, I've done some acting...he wore this bizarro hat and oversized tinted glasses that seemed like a costume. So I made sure not to look at him again directly and just focused on all the other rapt spectators.

The high from so successful an event is kick-ass, but it's also really tiring, at least once the high starts to wear off. The crowd started dissipating and the store managers let me know what a monetary and creative boon this had been for their location and the chain itself. The store's salaried employees were packing everything away and returning the store to normal; I had envisioned driving home after I was done, but I didn't feel like a six-hour trip through darkness right now. I whipped out my phone and searched through my booking app trying to find nearby digs that weren't full or outrageously expensive.

I was so immersed in my hunt and my filters that it really startled me when I suddenly heard a voice in front of me.

"Yellow."

"What?" I said automatically. It was Weird Beard Dude from the back row!

"Fourteen."

My synapses were firing too slowly to properly form a reaction. What the hell was this random shit this dude was spouting about? Did I need to hail one of the managers to come between us so I could get away?

"Fear of intimacy."

I squeezed my eyes shut for a few moments. Maybe

when I opened them he'd be gone.

"Favorite color, favorite number. Greatest fear?"

He wasn't gone. I tried to stay friendly, but my annoyance was showing for sure. "Um, look, can I help you with something?"

"Yeah," the guy said. "This. It's itchy as hell."

Just like that, the man reached under his chin and pulled at the waxy black beard. And pulled! And kept pulling! Until it came off!

Then he took off his dorky-ass hat and glasses.

Dafuq?

"Keith?"

He was clean-shaven, but it was most unmistakably him. I couldn't even process his being there. The only thing I could get out of my mouth was, "What did you do to your face?"

He rubbed a finger against its smooth skin. "I couldn't stick the fake beard on over my real one. Man, am I gonna get a rash from this thing."

"Why are you here? And in full-on espionage mode?"

He waved the beard. "Saw this on an episode of *Dynasty* once."

"More like *Duck Dynasty*."

"As for here...I heard you were going to be in town and I didn't want to run the risk of taking the focus off you like I ended up doing at that con in Redding."

Things were starting to make a little more sense – almost. "You live even further away from Boise than I do. You're telling me you drove, what – twelve hours? In disguise – "

"It was only seven – "

" – just to not take the focus off me. After the way I bit your head off last time you saw me."

"You gave Ozzy Osbourne a run for his money, that's for sure. Listen, about that...you weren't exactly...wrong about some things and I've been going over a lot of it since I saw you. I'd like to try to explain myself if I could."

Terrific. More excuses. "Dude, I thank you for coming out here on a mission and being a master of disguise and everything. But the store's going to close any minute and it's been a busy day. I'm super wiped."

"And hungry, I bet. I know how these events go – you probably didn't get a chance to eat. There's what looks like a decent Chinese restaurant next door. You wanna grab dinner?"

Keith was right about one thing. I had to eat. And I supposed it didn't matter at this point whether I had company or not when I did it. He wasn't going away and I didn't have the energy to fence with him. Oh, don't worry. No more goo-goo eyes for me where Keith Kirby was concerned. This would just be supping with an acquaintance. And from his pitch, maybe some actual closure – and answers – might be on the menu.

11

WE WALKED IN NEAR silence to the Chinese place. Obviously he had enough to say where he wasn't going to start en route and I really didn't have anything to say to him. I did have to chuckle, though, when we were being taken to our table and I realized he was still holding that ghastly fake beard in his hand. He saw the synthetic fuzz poking out from between his fingers and sheepishly shoved the thing in his pocket. I guess that broke my ice a little bit.

"I dunno," I offered, settling into the booth. "I kinda liked the real thing. So – yellow, eh?"

"My beard wasn't – " It took Keith a moment to remember his own codewords. "Oh! Yeah. Favorite color. More of a mustard yellow, really, or a gold. Like the kind we grew up with in the '70s."

"I never would have guessed you're an autumn," I wise-cracked. Banter remained light like this until after our orders were taken and we were left relatively alone. Then an awkward silence descended on us. Was he just waiting until the food arrived so we wouldn't be interrupted or overheard? For my part, I hadn't agreed to this breaking of fortune cookies just to sit here. "So," I forced myself to say. "What is this I wasn't exactly...wrong about?"

Keith took a breath, then stopped himself. "Suddenly now that I'm here this doesn't want to come out of my mouth," he admitted. "You know I have legitimate work pressures and keeping my career going takes up the bulk of my time. I'm not going to apologize for doing what I have to do to remain successful. But," he hesitated, "it is really easy to get swept up in it."

I nodded, squelching the urge to comment.

"You called me a flake back at Baltimore. That hurt, Brody. I don't mean to be flaky, I really don't. I mean well. But somehow I always end up having a hard time making space for people in my life. I can't tell you how often I've worried that I've done that with my kids. It never means I don't care, though. When I told you I cared about you, I meant it. When I told you I liked you, I meant it."

I couldn't help squaring my eyes. "Is that why you sandbagged us the first chance you got?"

"Quite frankly? Yes."

Wow. Wasn't expecting that level of bluntness.

"But it wasn't just you," he clarified. "I did need to pull back from even the thought of relationships. Everything had gotten so overwhelming. I told the other couple of guys I was dating I only wanted to be friends as well. I had to recalibrate. You can understand that, can't you?"

"I never said I couldn't," I answered quietly.

"There was another thing you said," Keith continued. "Not long after I closed the door on any romantic possibilities with you. In the vein of 'anyone who keeps themselves that busy is running from something'?"

"Oh, you *were* paying attention." I sighed and pulled in my claws. "Well, maybe it wasn't my place to play armchair psychiatrist...it's just that I've seen it before. My ex almost got off burning the candle at both ends when we first got together. The whole first year or so he barely made time for me. And he had a lot of his own issues he was running from, as I found out over the years. Not that I don't have my own that I run from, I assure you."

"Yeah, don't we all. Brody, the romantic turn things took with us caught me totally off guard. Sure, I was dating some fellas, but even that was kind of a big step for me. As I mentioned over our correspondence, I was married to my ex-wife for a long time and the coupla dudes I tried relationships with...well, they always turned into these big drama-filled ordeals. Then you came along. And you can be...a little intense."

A little eyeroll slipped out at that. "So I've been told," I half-smirked. "You have no idea how much I tried not to be...intense. I'm a man of my passions, I guess. I'm either all in or not at all. Haven't decided yet if that's a character flaw or just part of who I am. So I did freak you out over thinking you were going to Phoenix the city instead of Phoenix your employer and getting all 'don't bail on me' about it."

"That did spook me, yes. But I found myself trying to protect myself long before that."

"And...that's what you meant by fear of intimacy."

Keith offered a weak smile. "Keeping yourself maniacally busy is one way to avoid it, that's for sure." Looking to make sure our server wasn't coming with his Szechuan noodles and my beef and broccoli, he continued in a softer tone. "Work is easy. Art is just what I do. I've never had to question it. Interacting with the rest of the human race? Definitely scarier. I do find it difficult to get close to people. You know from our initial messaging that I've wrestled with some mental health stuff."

"That's part of the reason I felt comfortable with you right away." I raised my hand. "Some days I'm sure I'm the poster child for depression and anxiety. So I feel ya."

"Maybe *I* felt like I didn't want to subject you to it."

I just gave him a long look. "I would have understood."

He took his eyes off mine for a moment, then thought better of it, letting out a self-deprecating laugh. "I'm not very good at this. I express myself better through my charcoal and pens."

"For someone who doesn't have either handy, you're not doing too badly."

I got the feeling there might have been a little more there, but I knew it had taken some effort for him to voice this much, especially with the reminders of what was at his core. Dinner arrived and we moved on to less complicated topics, despite there remaining a tangible heaviness in the air between us. Still, it was all helping. I knew I had contributed to the way things had gone down between us, but for so long I had only a constant reexamination of my behavior to try and make sense out of it. That Keith had taken some responsibility and filled in some blanks did bring a level of peace about things I hadn't felt since the beginning of our friendship that never happened.

We pretty much ended up closing out the restaurant. "I'm wondering," Keith said. "You're not still planning on driving back to Reno tonight, are you?"

"Oh, God, no. In fact, your impromptu costume party interrupted my search for accommodations. Be interesting to see if there are any vacancies left at this late hour." I pulled my phone back out to see how accurate that was, but Keith stopped me.

"I, uh...already have a room down the street. Two beds, don't worry."

I couldn't help but smile a little. "That...probably wouldn't be entirely appropriate. Wouldn't be the first hotel in our repertoire, though."

"Oh, San Francisco."

"I was more thinking about botched Baltimore." I didn't know if I should ask the question that popped into my mind next. "Um, that business of us not seeing each other there after we'd planned on it for weeks...that wasn't part of you protecting yourself, was it?"

Keith looked genuinely surprised. "Where'd you get that idea? No. It really was a comedy of errors. Between someone stealing your pass and then my damn phone dying...not being able to leave the table and find a place to charge it...wow. I only went to the hotel because I couldn't call you, and believe me, I walked around looking for you. I just got so exhausted I had to get some sleep, and I figured you'd left, anyway. Sure was surprised when you showed up on my door!"

"That whole thing was super surreal," I nodded as I scanned my booking app again, glad to have the confirmation that Ms. Hypnosis had been full of shit, at least about that. I didn't bother asking if Keith's son's accident was real. I knew Keith wouldn't have made that up, but I figured you were wondering. I found a pricey but available place and snagged it. However, in doing so, I felt like now I was doing the ignoring. "Keith, I want you to know something. I really *do* appreciate your coming out here and delving into this stuff. It filled in a lot of blanks I needed filled. I guess you must be pretty tired, too, huh."

He shrugged a little. "Now that you mention it."

"Tell you what. Why don't I walk you to your hotel, and then...uh...um...I guess I'll be seeing you in all the old familiar social media places, to paraphrase the song."

"Yeah."

"Yeah."

Okay, this got awkward. But things felt like they'd come to a natural conclusion. Keith seemed to struggle with a single word. "Unless..."

I was genuinely curious. "Unless what?"

"Well...are you in a hurry to drive home tomorrow? Maybe we could hang out part of the day first. I mean, we're already here...and who knows when we might have another opportunity."

Hmm.

Yeah, yeah, yeah. I hadn't forgotten the obstacle course I'd run trying to get the slightest bit of communication out of him. Okay, I now had a better understanding of why he'd ghosted me. But it couldn't just be forgive and forget over fried rice and wontons.

I thought about it, and it was hard to argue his point. We probably *wouldn't* have a chance like this again. And it wasn't like I had to be anywhere at a set time the next day.

Why the hell not. Maybe there was still a friendship to salvage here. I told him to give me a call in the morning.

What I didn't tell him was, if tomorrow came and he reverted to form, I wasn't going to wait around. I'd give him 'til check-out time at noon and then it was *hasta la vista, baby.*

Sorry, Ah-nold. I was thinking strictly Jody Watley here.

12

THE NEXT MORNING I was jolted out of a sound sleep by my phone's cool alien sound effect ringtone. It was Keith! Well, no need to Ah-nold or Jody Watley him, then; I just wasn't going to sound as coherent as I might have with another couple hours' rest and a shower.

He thought we might get some breakfast and then walk around the downtown core. Along with pancakes and bacon and scrambled eggs came a lot of breeze-shooting. How his latest project was going, how his kids were, how his home renovations were coming along. Naturally he still had a lot on the ball in terms of his comic cons and the associated racking up of frequent flier miles. But he did note that he was trying to keep things from getting as crazy as they did when we'd failed at getting together last summer. He said he saw reason for attempting more balance in his life. I toasted him with my toast for that.

I somehow didn't have as much to talk about, at least in terms of my life as it stood – heavy promotion with "our" book continued, which took up a good deal of time. However, as I mentioned before, I was myself working to carve out space for friends and self-improvement. I didn't get into details with him about the heart opening stuff. Didn't seem necessary somehow.

As we slowly ticked toward afternoon, we did in fact take a stroll through downtown Boise, commenting on the architecture and other little touches that gave the town its identity. We made our way down to the Boise River and enjoyed the fresh air neither of us probably got enough of. Though our chat was easy, it didn't feel as easy as the one we had when we first met; in fact, I couldn't help sensing a wall between us as we talked. On later examination I had to concede I was probably more its builder than him. For whatever self-protection he had engaged in, I suppose I was doing a little of that myself here. Hell, not eighteen hours ago I was laboring under the impression that Keith belonged in the annals of history. I never expected to be playing tourist with him, now or ever.

Along the river there was this sweet little park, complete with playground equipment. Since it was a weekday, the kiddies were presumably in school and the new mothers with their strollers and the elderly folks communing together were ignoring the slides and the jungle gyms. Not me! I guess I'm just a big kid at heart; I've never gone in for that too-old-for-this-or-that bullshit. I beckoned Keith to join me on the swings. Feeling that little rush going back and forth was quite freeing.

I dunno. Something about us being little boys together cut a good swath through my resistance. I got a little more chatty. And I realized something. We were actually getting to know each other – the way I had wanted to before that ill-fated comic con in Baltimore and those wearying weeks afterwards. Ironic, right? A little too ironic – and yeah I really do think! (Thank you

Alanis Morrissette.) Still, better late than never was kind of nice.

The youthful surroundings also worked to change the tone of our conversation. We actually did get into childhood stuff. He told me what it was like for him growing up in Montana. He was the nerdy kid who got laughed at. I could understand. I had been the gay kid who didn't know he was gay who got laughed at.

We both sat atop the slide. There was no way two grown men would both fit down it, but there was that whimsical possibility we might try. You could better see across the river to the other side of Boise from our perch and the mild air felt good and we were sitting close enough together I could feel his warmth. Something about that combination conspired to get my wall down quite a bit further.

"You know, I have a greatest fear, too," I started. "I mean, fair is fair. Trite as it sounds, I have a fear of abandonment. I don't know exactly where it comes from. I would have assumed from my parents' divorce, but I'm pretty sure I felt that special kind of panic long before that. I never did have a lot of friends. The few I had, I was always afraid they'd want to hang out with someone else eventually. Maybe that's why I got anxious when you didn't write back right away – and definitely why I made an idiot of myself out of that whole Phoenix thing. I guess I just wanted you to know that...you're not the only one who's afraid."

He reached over and gripped my arm reassuringly. There was a certain comfort between us here, the one that only comes from getting real with someone. Then he offered up this verbal response:

"Race you to the bottom!"

He lurched ahead of me and slid down; I was right behind him by two feet. He managed to quickly stand up once he got to the bottom, but in my zest I barrelled right into him, knocking him down. And there we were, lying in the sand at the bottom of a kiddie slide, laughing our fool heads off.

It was getting into mid-afternoon and we each still had a long haul looming in front of us. We walked back to the IHOP where our cars were parked. It was like our first meeting in that there was this definite sense neither of us wanted to leave the other. That was the only parallel I was going to allow, though. No more confessions of adorability here.

"It was good spending time with you," Keith smiled. "I hope we can do it again sometime."

"Hmm," I said half-jokingly, half-sarcastically. "Where I have I heard that before..."

"Look, I meant it before and I mean it – " Keith caught his defensiveness. "Brody, I really did want a friendship with you. Now that I've gotten a taste of it...well, I think you'll be hearing from me more often."

I took a long look at him and let out a slow breath. "I really want to give you the benefit of the doubt here." I stood there, my feet planted, weighing the present moment against the months that loomed behind us. "All right. Let's see how you do with follow-through this time. I mean, I don't expect to be at the top of any of your lists or anything. But I'm not gonna chase you. I will do my best to reply sooner than later if and when you reach out. If you don't...well, that'll be on you, Kirby."

Keith looked both amused and respectful at the same time. "Well, you certainly told me."

I stepped back and made a show of indicating myself. "You coulda had all this, buddy!" I added, slapping a hand on my tummy that needed slimming.

I waved him toward me, and we relaxed into a very warm hug. "It was good spending time with you, too," I nearly whispered.

We each opened our car doors. "Send me a message that you got home okay," Keith asked. "And I'll do the same."

As I USB'd my phone into my car's entertainment system so I could have my tunes, I watched Keith drive away.

"Well, that's the end of that," I told myself.

13

NOT LONG AFTER I got back to Reno, my phone showed me a one-line notification that Keith had arrived home in one piece. Fighting against my usual verbosity, I acknowledged his message with a few well-chosen words and even held off on the emoji. I *had* enjoyed our time together. More than I was going to let myself feel or articulate, even to myself. But I wasn't going to set myself up for disappointment with him again. I just wasn't.

A day passed. Then two. Then three. Just as I anticipated, no Keith. I knew how this scene played out; I'd seen the movie a couple of times. It was at least good that we'd had a chance to talk finally; maybe now I could truly put our brief chapter to bed and move on.

I forget what God created on the fourth day, but on this fourth day, guess who I heard from? Well, if you've read this far you know it had to be Keith. He'd had to get right back to work upon returning to his world, but he wanted to thank me for the colorful bruise my shoe had given his leg coming down the slide in Boise. Also, he felt he'd gotten the short end of the stick because I hadn't divulged to him what my own favorite color and number were during our hours together.

I had to smile to myself. I left his message unanswered for a while, trying to maintain the new less-anxious vibe.

But when I finally replied we ended up having a nice he-said-he-said for twenty minutes. Couldn't really ask for more than that. And I didn't.

To my surprise, these keyboarded convos started happening more often. None of them were overly long, yet with each one Keith shared more about himself, and, as I'd vowed to put my money where my mouth was in terms of participation, I let him see further into the Brody world as well. I finally found out his freakin' middle name. It's Allen. (Mine is Connor, by the way.)

About a month out from our playground playdate, I had gotten used to Keith's communiqués. For the most part, I was letting him do the initiating; I figured that was the only way I could know for sure he was into this friendship. I wasn't trying to play games, mind you. Given what I'd been through before with him, let's call it..."quality control."

I liked our newfound friendship. I was even up front about the fact that I'd finally submitted that dating profile and had met two or three guys for coffee. Another I went on a couple of dates with. No, I wasn't trying to rub it in Keith's face. It's just where I was. He still talked about staying pulled back from romance; there was never anything beyond platonic in our screen chats and I wasn't going to go there, either. But a guy gets lonely.

And while we're on that...confession time. I ended "the drought". The dude I dated...he was cute and...well, you know how you always know right away if you're attracted to someone but sometimes it takes you a little while to figure out whether or not there's a basis for anything? This guy, I think we both knew we weren't each others' type relationship-wise, but I felt comfortable with him and one thing led to another. No, I wasn't going back on what I said about no hookups. At least I knew him a little and our night together was surprisingly intimate for what it was. I was sure he would make someone an amazing boyfriend. It just couldn't be me. For what it's worth, that experience reminded me that my sexuality was alive and kicking. Something I had sometimes forgotten through years of barren deserts.

I didn't tell Keith it had rained. Or the fact that...I mean, these guys were nice and everything. They just weren't Keith. Whoever was going to capture my heart was going to have to be something really special. Coming as close as I had with Keith confirmed that.

Keith did his travelling and I found myself being much better about his gaps in messages. Probably because I wasn't as invested as I'd been during our first getting-to-know-you go-round. It wasn't like I didn't have my own career to keep me busy. I'm not gonna lie, though – I started looking forward to those bings that meant he'd sent a note. We continued on with our pleasantries, but also started digging deeper more often, getting a better idea of what made the other tick.

One day he threw me for a complete and total loop. He had found out about a comic con in Salt Lake City the following month which was about equidistant between us. Did I want to go in on a table with him? Not only could we split vendor fees and hold down the fort when the other needed to hit the head, he said, it would be a great way of introducing my work to his fan base given his connection to it. Plus, we'd get a chance to see each other. It would be a hoot.

A do-over comic con? We were 0-for-2 on that score, so I was all about it. I did relish the idea of reaching new readers. But I told him in return I would absolutely be willing to help him with setting up, transactions, whatever. He couldn't have agreed more enthusiastically, and as the days got closer, he suggested we get on the horn so we could settle up logistics.

Well, well. Our first phone call since before everything went south. I know; I shouldn't still have been thinking about that. Actually, where we were at now was much better and I wouldn't have traded it for the hoping and anxiety and longing that had come with last year's interactions. I really was starting to feel like I could call Keith a friend, and not just an acquaintance, as I had labeled him during Baltimore's dust-up.

So, the phone thing happened. A lot of it was who was going to meet who where and how much did I owe you and how do you want to handle social media. There also had been the matter of whether or not our individual publishers were on board, but we were each able to confirm that they actually thought a joint event was a good idea. After all, it wasn't just a matter of me being exposed to Keith's audience, but him being exposed to mine.

Once we got all the bookkeeping out of the way, we did yap for a while about various and sundry. His son was finally done with physical therapy and had made a full recovery. His daughter had just gotten accepted to a university. And his favorite band was doing a reunion tour. Oh! But he almost forgot! What were we going to do about lodging? It wouldn't really make sense for us to get two rooms.

I admit, I had kind of avoided the subject myself, though not entirely consciously. The first time we were alone in a hotel room, I had to tamp down thoughts of him and the bed and of course my "adorable" admission had led to all kinds of ups and downs. The second time we were both exhausted and if it had been any more platonic the concierge would have brought us purity rings. But yeah – doubling the expense wasn't very prudent. We could just as easily share a double room, each have our own bed, and now that we were all friendly it would be kind of fun to bunk together.

Oh, come on. Is your mind in the gutter again? Okay, maybe mine was, too – a little. I still found Keith attractive, and maybe in some ways he was even more so because of our recent closeness. But that wasn't going to happen. It was very clear we were friends and that's all we were going to be. I would not open this whole thing up again.

Sharing a hotel room with Keith Kirby. What had I gotten myself into?

14

PROBABLY SHOULD HAVE FLOWN to Salt Lake City, but imagine the extra you have to pay for schlepping several heavy boxes of books onto an airplane these days. Next they'll charge you to use the bathroom. Anyway, while I could have slept on the plane (sort of), the long drive was cheaper, even if it gave my brain more time to try and interject off-topic stuff about Keith.

I wasn't really sure what to expect at this con. Not even so much because of Keith – it was because I usually went to cons and book events as a solo act. Come to think of it, a lot of my life had kind of been a solo act. And I didn't know what I would do if stuff went down like Redding and I just sat there while all the attention got heaped on him. Again, he deserved his accolades. It's just awkward. But you know me by now – freak out first, ask questions later.

My GPS led me to the hotel he had booked, a cozy little place off the Interstate and within walking distance to the convention center. Which was good – remember how crazy parking was at Baltimore? We'd certainly have to drive to the venue to unload our stuff and set up, though.

I knocked on his room's door as I had done twice before. What was it about us and hotels?

He was super psyched to see me. Gave me a great big hug, which was a little shaggier than it had been the last time I saw him.

"Back for a command performance, eh?" I noted, indicating his face.

He gave his renewed beard a tug. "You did say you kinda liked it."

No, Brody, don't be stupid, I scolded myself. *He did not grow his beard back for you. Now would you get to work already?* So we did. While we weren't able to park as close to the venue entrance as we would have liked, we saw to the task of loading in our equipment and merch without complaint. It was kind of nice – and novel – to not have to do all the prep by myself. He gave me a hand and certainly I jumped in and helped him, especially with him having more setting up to do than I did. Sometimes I could feel my heart pounding. Had to be because I wasn't used to this much prolonged exercise.

I wanted to check out one of the fast food joints I don't have at home, and since we had an early morning coming Keith agreed that the expediency would be an acceptable trade-off for the calories and cholesterol. We weren't overly chatty, but that seemed more because we'd both had long drives and then gotten a workout. Sleep would be most definitely welcome.

It wasn't until we got up to the room that it really hit me we were going to be spending the night in close proximity. As he waltzed out of the bathroom in his T-shirt and shorts brushing his teeth I had this flash that said *This is what it would be like if you were together.* If Keith hadn't been ten feet away from me I might literally have bitch slapped myself. I shouldn't have had to keep reminding my brain to stay in its lane and shut up. Sure, I suppose it was only human to have thoughts like that. Damn it.

We sat up a little and went over a general game plan for the next day, then ventured into sillier stuff. That was fine because I was really too tired to go too deep, much less reveal any discomfort I might be having about our accommodations. We set our alarms and hugged each other good night, and I could still feel his warmth when I lay down to sleep. Or try. For the first hour or so I found myself just lying awake watching *him* sleep. It was a lot like that con in Baltimore. Only everything had changed since then. We were developing a nice camaraderie; in that sense we were closer and I wasn't feeling that terrible unrequited desire. Still, even after he turned away I kept my eyes on him until I was finally able to drift off.

The next thing I knew, it was morning. Keith was rarin' to go and found my unconscious yawning humorous. "See, this is why it never would have worked out," I joked, perhaps because I wasn't fully awake and neither was my filter. But the convention-goers were lined out the door and duty called, so I forced myself to work through the fog until it lifted.

It was actually a lot of fun! Like I told you, people hadn't been as aware of my book as they were of Keith's work, but lots of folks got excited about it upon seeing Keith's cover and hearing his ringing endorsements. He'd actually read it and knew how to tease just enough of the story to entice potential readers and not give anything major away. Conversely, my effusiveness about Keith's art converted a few on-the-fence attendees.

But it wasn't just that. We had a nice symbiosis going, and it made the whole merry uproar a lot more enjoyable. When he was up to his eyeballs in autographs I manned his credit card reader or got photos with him and eager fans. He turned the camera around on me at times and shifted books out of boxes when the on-table stock got low and I was busy with a sales pitch. I made sure his phone was charged. He unexpectedly brought me soda on his way back from the bathroom.

And then there were the moments where people wanted photos and videos of us together and outright interviewed us on the spot. We discoursed professionally but also told a lot of jokes and laughed a lot. The convention people even shot footage of us for their web site and the local paper stopped by for a chat, getting snaps of us that they forwarded to us immediately. Keith and I both posted the best shot to our followers. I was damn proud. So much so it made it easier to stave off the memory of that first picture we'd taken together that night when we'd –

Yeah! So it was a hectic but satisfying day. I don't know how Keith would rate his take but based on my experiences I was making money hand over fist. We got back to the room and plopped down on our respective beds, going Dutch on a pizza and watching a little TV before turning in. And there was another hug – hearty, inviting. Did it last a few seconds longer than it presumably should have? Never mind. It felt good and we were becoming buddies and that's a level of fulfillment all unto itself.

Yet I wasn't unaware I was starting to sound like a broken record to myself.

The second half of the con went much like the first. Busy, not a lot of time for small talk but once again being each others' helpmates. We were partners at this event, pure and simple. It never bothered me that Keith drew the bigger crowd. I was happy to assist, and for his part, he never left me paddling when I got swamped, either. And are you ready for this? I actually ran out of books. As in sold out. Typically I can gauge how many to bring, though more often than not I end up bringing a bunch home. Not this time! Keith joined me in assuring disappointed fans copies could still be obtained elsewhere and pointing them to my social media accounts.

At several moments during the day, he'd stop and do quick sketches for his bigger devotees (for a nominal fee, natch). Every time, I became mesmerized by how he could take a blank piece of paper and turn it into something living in a matter of a couple of minutes.

After he sent one such happy recipient away and we had a break in the action, I asked him, "How do you do that?"

"Do what?"

"Turn out these incredible drawings so effortlessly. I mean, I like to think I have my share of talents, but I can't draw worth a crap. Does that just come naturally or did you have to study for years?"

As you might expect, it was a little of both: he'd begun creating pretty much as soon as he could hold a pencil and went on to hone his talent at art school.

He pooh-poohed it; drawing was as much a part of him as breathing and had been as far back as he could remember.

I shook my head admiringly and indicated the mob around us. "They're lucky to have something personalized from you. It's quite the memento."

Something interesting happened over those two days. I discovered I wasn't mad at him anymore. I guess what had hurt more than him not seeing me as romantic potential was losing him completely for months, having him disappear out of my life unable to even be friends with him. This had certainly healed that, as had his efforts the since my book event in Boise. It was like all was right with the world. And I could accept that this was how it was supposed to be, us being friends.

Well, the day ended. Then began the daunting task of packing everything up and lugging it out to our cars. Admittedly, I had less to worry about because all my merch was gone and it was just a matter of getting the display stuff loaded. He had quite a bit more to play Tetris with, if only because he had a much wider variety of comics and other collectibles that had to go home with him. I played roadie for him and the joviality between us continued. Up until the very last, we were a team.

But you know, all good things. I had spotted another fast food chain we don't have in Reno. I had practically been able to taste those wonderfully greasy fish and chips all afternoon. Keith arched an eyebrow.

"What, too artery-hardening for you?" I smiled.

"Partially," he concurred. "But this was a big con for both of us – especially you; they cleaned you out! Don't you think that's worthy of something more...celebratory?"

I supposed grease didn't have to be the word that day. I nodded approvingly as I moved to close his car's hatchback.

"Actually..."

He hesitated for a moment. It was like he was suddenly lost in thought. "Actually..." I coaxed.

"Well, it's just that I heard about this to-die-for Italian restaurant up the road about a mile or so. Apparently they have the best chicken carbonara this side of Napoli. I think we should try it out."

"Fattening Italian food? I'm down," I told him.

"And...I'd like you to go there with me...as my date."

I just about fell into a dead faint right there in the parking garage.

I had no idea what to say. Between the part of me I'd tried to hide even from myself doing a happy jig and the part of me that had worked so hard to just think of Keith as a friend, my mouth completely short-circuited.

"Date?" I finally choked out, adding stupidly, "Me?"

Keith offered up a nervous but genuine chuckle. "Well, I'm not asking the parking attendant."

I sucked in an involuntary deep breath and regained just enough composure for one disjointed sentence. "I, uh...I mean...it's just...you know, like they say...um...this is so... sudden."

"Not really. I've been thinking about it for a while now. You gonna turn a guy down?"

Come on, Brody, focus. "I'm just trying to get my head around..." The focus kicked in. "What changed your mind?"

"Something you wrote me after I closed the door

on getting to know you and seeing where things might lead: I never did give it much of a chance. Now this past little while we've been becoming friends and not just... acquaintances" – I bristled a little remembering how angrily I'd labeled us that after we ran into each other in Redding – "well, you know...it's dinner. Not a lifetime commitment." He looked at me encouragingly.

If there were other people in the garage, I didn't notice them. I realized I had never closed his hatchback and my arm was still raised to do so with my hand placed just below his license plate. How is it I notice strange stuff in moments like this? It was just a meal he was offering, and it wasn't like we hadn't already shared a few of those. But a dinner date? After all the turmoil and longing and vacillating emotions? Did I really want to open myself up to another round of that?

Damn the hypnotherapist. I could hear her words in my head. Wasn't opening myself up specifically what she had been beckoning me to do? Wasn't setting my heart free what she said would make it possible for me to draw in its desires for success, for fulfillment, for love? Here the man I had been trying so hard to forget wanted another chance. He'd really been doing his best to make up for ghosting me. We knew each other far better than when I'd wanted to date him the first time. Could I really say no to this?

I gave his hatchback a gentle slam; the resulting echo snapped me out of my contemplation. "*Bene*," I replied wryly. "That's about the extent of my Italian."

"Maybe it won't be by the end of the dessert course."

15

AFTER I SHEEPISHLY CONVINCED Keith we should run back to the hotel for a minute because the con and its dismantling had me sweaty and dirty, we headed to the restaurant he had chosen while secretly planning to ask me out. He had not been led astray. Everything about the place was top-notch and felt like it was tailor-made for the auspicious moment I wouldn't have dreamed possible two hours ago.

"This sauce," I commented with mind blown, "is so good that if I'd ever wanted children, I'd name my first-born after it."

"'Carbonara Rohan'," Keith laughed quietly. "Your kid might have trouble getting through school with that one."

I wondered for a moment if I'd stuck my foot in it. "No offense about children, of course," I acknowledged. "It's just I never saw myself as a parent. I can't even imagine what that must be like, raising two children – and having them grown-up now!"

"It's corny as hell to say," Keith observed, rolling his eyes. "But they're better creations than anything I've ever drawn."

"How did they take it when you came out?"

"That was the part I had been most worried about.

And it ended up being the part I'd least needed to worry about. My ex-wife was another matter, as you can understand" – I nodded – "but Joseph and Claudia were really cool about it. Kids this century...they're much more accepting about sexual orientation. A lot more than I was about my own those first few years. You?"

It didn't take much to reach back. "I think I knew I was gay in kindergarten, really," I explained. "Just that young I had no words to describe my feelings. Some still say it's not biological...but I would seriously beg to differ based on my own experience."

Keith elaborated on the couple of "drama-filled" relationships he'd had with guys once he'd recovered from ending his marriage and its ensuing fallout. I could see why he had been gun-shy with me before. Both guys sounded pretty volatile...one of them had gotten physical a few times.

"Maybe I brought it on being busy so much, I don't know," Keith surmised.

"No, there's no excuse for that."

"You mean you didn't feel like chucking something at me when I took so long to respond to your heartfelt admissions?"

"Let's not go that far," I smirked. "Kidding, of course." By way of comparison, I added, "There's no denying I've had drama in my life – a lot of it I created. But most of it is internal now. Unlike the old days, things are pretty chill outwardly." I hadn't quite verbalized that before and realized I was rather fortunate.

I got the feeling the waiter knew we were in the midst of a special night. He brought an extra candle for our table and anyone new who came in, he seated far enough away from us that we could still enjoy some privacy. The sound of organettos lilted out of the ceiling's speakers.

Keith caught me smiling. "Are you thinking the same thing I am? That Mario is expecting us to partake of the same noodle?"

"Oh, God," I said in mock horror. "Which one of us is the lady and which one is the tramp?"

He swallowed exaggeratedly. "I plead the Fifth."

"You know, I can't help thinking back to that first meal we shared in San Fran. It felt so much like a first date and I didn't dare say that to you. And now here we are, on an actual first date...I'm still not sure what to make of it all. How to reconcile the fantasy versus the reality."

"But are you enjoying yourself?"

Beams of light shone through my crumbling wall. "Yes." Then the next thing that popped into my head slipped out. "But La Cucina? 'The Kitchen'? Couldn't Mario have come up with a more original name for a restaurant than that?" I winked.

Keith just gave me the warmest look. "What am I going to do with you."

It had been a very full day between the con and the surprise date, so we decided we should head back to our room. Ever the smart-ass, I piped up with, "Look at you. One date and you're taking me to a hotel."

He put the key in the door knowingly. "Well, we both just happen to live here for the time being. What, you never ended up in a hotel room after a first date?"

I cleared my throat. "I'm a prude – but I'm not dead."

Keith turned the lights on and held out an arm. "May I walk you to your bed, sir?"

"You goofball. Oh! Wait, wait, wait."

I ran to the other end of the room near the bathroom. "Okay. Now."

Keith pursed his lips in amusement and came to meet me, taking my arm. We strolled across the overly-colorful carpet like we were dandies at the height of Victorian society. By the time we actually got to my bed we were in fits of laughter.

The way Keith was looking at me...it was like that first night. Like we had come full circle.

Keith must have been thinking it, too. As then, he touched my face. "You remember how this all started? With you telling me you thought I was adorable?"

I could barely breathe. "I couldn't not."

"Well, I've finally come to one inescapable conclusion."

"Which is?"

"You're pretty adorable yourself." I was dizzy from having him so near as our lips met again for the first time in what had felt like forever. It was the same in that what he was communicating through his kiss was so gentle and loving. But there was more in it this time, too. I stroked his hair and let myself give in, his beard brushing against me, wanting to dissolve completely into the softness of his mouth.

Being a man of my passions as I've described, emotions welled up in me and threatened to bubble up through my eyes. Keith seemed to notice the involuntary shudder that came with it.

"Hey...are you crying?"

I was thoroughly embarrassed. But it was what it was. “Yeah,” I admitted, wiping away a tear that had escaped.

Keith seemed like he didn’t know what to think. “Was it that bad?” he tried to joke.

“Oh, my Lord, no,” I assured quickly. “I was just remembering our first kiss and how everything felt so promising in that moment, only to fall through, and then how I tried so hard to forget you when this was what I wanted...and then being friends and having to push any romantic thought that came up out of my mind...”

“Sad tears?”

“Just a few. I guess it’s just a release from holding so much back for so long.”

Keith was caring and introspective. “I guess I did put you through the wringer, didn’t I.”

“But they’re happy tears, too, Keith! Everything I had thought about you from when you kissed me before, the reasons I’d started developing feelings for you to begin with...it’s like that was all confirmed just now, like I didn’t imagine it.”

He tapped my nose with his finger. “That’s a lot of breakdown for one kiss.”

I glanced at the floor shyly, smiling. “Yeah, well... welcome to my world.”

He guided my face back up so we were looking right into each others’ eyes. “In that case...I wonder what happens if I kiss you again?”

He didn’t have to wonder. Neither of us did. I allowed myself to junk any further analysis and just be in the moment, this wonderful moment. Words weren’t necessary anymore, either. We stood there, his hands slipped around my waist and mine caressing his back as our lips searched each other for who could tell how long.

I don't remember how we got there, but at one point I became aware we had sat down on my bed. We had gotten a little more playful. Tongues intertwined and his lips and whiskers brushed against my ear, then my neck. It would have been easy...so easy. But...

We were gazing at each other and holding both hands in front of us. "What are you thinking?" Keith asked me.

"Just that I'm awfully glad you grew your beard back," I teased. "And that you've been taking an active role in our friendship...and now this."

Keith kissed my forehead. "You did say you weren't going to chase me."

"Please don't get me wrong – it's not that I want to be chased, either. Or, um...chaste. I'm not wearing one of those belts under my pants or anything. That's not what's stopping me from...I really would like to...it's just now doesn't seem...you know? Man, you must think I'm a terrible tease."

"Oh, yes, the absolute worst," Keith deadpanned. "Hey, despite what you're arousing in me here, I'm not quite ready myself. Plus I'm way too tired! Gone are the days I could just turn it on at a moment's notice."

"I hear ya on that one. I'm pretty zonked, too. In a good way, but zonked. Thanks for understanding."

"So...think any of this merits a second date?"

I wet my lip thoughtfully. "I believe I do feel such a sequel is merited. We'll have to figure out the geography, I guess, if you..."

"If I don't ghost you again?'"

"Sorry. Knee-jerk reaction. I should be giving you more credit than that at this point."

"If the situation were reversed, I'd probably be thinking it, too."

"Well, if we truly are going to explore things," I mused, "let's keep the channels of communication open this time. Really open. Like if the need to protect yourself comes up, if fear grips you again, that's okay. But let's at least talk about it."

"Yeah, I guess it's like when you have a fear of flying. Sometimes you just have to get on that airplane and...fly."

"That's a good analogy."

"Well," Keith said, releasing my hands and stretching, "it seems to me this is an overnight flight. And since we're choosing not to join the Mile High Club, perhaps I could interest you in bunking with me in first class? It's got everything you don't have in coach. Super deluxe pillows, a cushy blanket – "

"I seem to recall the flight attendant providing me with those."

" – and my arms around you all night."

"Oh!" I couldn't get the little smirk off my face. "Yes, in that respect coach is decidedly lacking."

Brushing our teeth and getting into our night clothes – this time without having to take turns in the bathroom – I found myself as excited to cuddle with Keith as I would have been to have sex. I didn't expect I was going to get much sleep, though. As we climbed into his bed I knew I would want to soak up every moment. I hadn't spooned with a guy in what felt like decades. His arms were strong and he kissed the back of my neck. "Good night to you, Mr. Rohan."

I had one last moment of animation. "Hey! I remember some Italian I forgot I knew. *Bella notte.* That's been going through my head for hours, since the restaurant."

"*What* a dog." I could hear the smile in Keith's voice behind me as he quoted the movie.

I called it. I only occasionally drifted off in his sturdy embrace, feeling his breath on my neck.

It was the loveliest way to not be able to sleep I could think of.

16

WHEN KEITH AND I woke up entangled in each other, there was a sense of surrealism to it. But we'd really gone on a first date. We'd really kissed, and it wasn't just another one of my detailed fantasies. It was real. He was holding me against his chest. Neither of us wanted to get out of that bed. Alas, checkout time was looming closer and closer, imposing on us to get a move on.

I was almost scared to say anything. I felt like the slightest word would pop the bubble we had spent the last several hours in, like losing its rainbowy sheen might make the world outside it unbearable. We got dressed and checked the weather reports for and on the way to our respective destinations. We kicked around the idea of breakfast but we both had a long way to go and things to take care of. Was this the way it was going to end?

I almost had a knot in my stomach as we walked to our cars with our suitcases rolling behind us. When we parted the first time in San Francisco, I had been so full of hope for the possibilities that lay before us. Now I found myself much more circumspect. Helluva note, right? Before I'd been willing to go whole hog based on essentially one kiss with a stranger; here I was leaving a friend who had become a borderline lover, and I was hesitant. I'm never what I should be.

Keith was kind of quiet, too. Maybe that's what was sending my defenses up. Yet he didn't seem hesitant when he kissed me goodbye and told me he'd miss me. No wonder I was all over the place. I didn't want to leave him. I was already afraid we'd never have another moment like this.

We got into our cars. He rolled down his passenger window and honked for me to roll down my driver's side. "Let me know you got home okay," came his request.

"You too."

And hey...*buongiorno*, dog," he winked. Hmm. A reference to last night for the road?

Speeding along the highway, I felt like I should have been flying without the plane given everything that had happened. A very lucrative weekend, a wider cross-section of people knowing about my book, and spending a romantic evening with a man I had longed for. I was having trouble assimilating it. I'd gone into the Salt Lake con thinking of Keith as a friend and that nothing could ever go past that, yet I'd come out of it with so many old feelings reawakened, and new ones born. And where she stops, nobody knows.

I had to give myself a little kick in the ass, too. What had happened between us was beautiful! The dinner, the kisses, the cuddling...even if nothing developed beyond that, there was a lot to be grateful for in just having had the experience, in getting to feel so good again. So I sent a silent thank-you to the ether and tried to remember to not close my heart again out of fear, whether Keith was in my future or not.

I rolled into my driveway and grabbed my phone to

notify him of my safe arrival. Just kept it short and light. Damn, it's hard to send a text and not expect an instant answer, isn't it? Ah, the advent of technology.

About twenty-five minutes later, I received a reply that he had likewise gotten home in one piece. I was going to let it go at that. No sense in seeming too eager. Gawd. Flashbacks to the day after our first meeting, or what?

I was getting ready to pop in some laundry before bed when my phone lit up again. It was Keith.

Turns out this 'notte' isn't as 'bella' without you.

This was most definitely progress.

Over the next few weeks, his schedule filled up as his regimen of comic cons were kicking in again. This time I was determined to be more chill. It didn't turn out to be all that necessary. Our chats and texts continued and Keith found time to resume phone calls, both at home and using that sketchy Bluetooth from his car, which by this point had become a running joke.

We even tried something new for us – a video chat. Hey, welcome to the 21st century! I was more nervous than I needed to be. He'd already seen how I looked when I woke up and my hair made me seem like a red-headed Tina Turner. Still, there were no romantic declarations from him and I wasn't going to coax any out of him, nor make any myself. I guess I had kind of been hoping to hear some, but then again, there was more to deepening our connection than sweet nothings. I just was having a hard time taking the temperature of our interactions. And as the weeks passed I started to think maybe the romantic stuff had fizzled out again, this time not from a lack of communication but because of the distance between us.

Then came the day he wanted to know if I had any space in my calendar coming up, a space big enough it would allow me to come out to Bozeman to see him. It would take me a full day to drive across Nevada and Idaho and a full day back, but he said we still had a meritorious second date to attend to if I wanted. I did want. I think I said something like "I thought you'd never ask," and I wasn't lying. I'd gotten back to my life but when we seemed to settle back into friendship I didn't want to push anything like I had before. At least this time we hadn't lost touch, so I hadn't worried about it as much.

I found the requested block of time. Despite the spike in sales and social media presence after the Salt Lake City con, the hype about my book was dying down and there wasn't much else I could do to promote it that I hadn't already done. I was starting to think maybe it was time to write something new. So I happened to have a little extra time on my hands. I allowed myself to look forward to the trip. Keith had said he wanted to show me around the burg he had called home the last two decades or so. Having Googled it, Bozeman looked like it could be really beautiful.

I wasn't disappointed, at least not in that. He took me for a drive in the surrounding mountains and played me some of his favorite songs in the car, including bootleg live versions he'd gotten a hold of. We stopped at this campground and took a little hike into the backwoods. The trail ended at this stunning waterfall. It was breathtaking.

Yet I couldn't completely enjoy the beauty. See, after I got to his house late the previous night, Keith hugged me and kissed me on the forehead. We heated up some soup and then he put me on the couch for the night. What was I missing? We hadn't gotten hot and heavy during our SLC meeting at my own behest, so I wasn't expecting anything like that now, or at least right away. But I did figure we'd resume the warm and fuzzy.

We sat down on a tree that had obviously fallen decades ago, conveniently right across a spring rushing by below us. Keith seemed pensive. I didn't like the vibe I was getting. Surely he didn't have me drive all the way out to Montana just to break things off?

"I feel pretty bad," he started. "I, uh, broke a promise to you. Or at least I didn't follow through on something we talked about. I...have felt myself freezing up again. But it's not you. Please know that."

"All right," I conceded, not knowing where this was going.

"I already started feeling it that last morning when we woke up together. Being with you was so awesome and I gotta tell ya...part of me really wanted you. A certain part, especially."

Leave it to me to find humor in the most inopportune moments. "You mean your visit to Morningwood Manor? That was a little har – er, difficult not to notice."

"So much for keeping that secret," Keith smiled thinly. "But I wasn't going to act on it. I fully respected the fact you weren't ready, and – "

"Hey, for what it's worth, if I hadn't been so comatose, I...probably could have gone for it in that moment myself.

Is this what you mean by freezing up? Because it kinda sounds like the opposite."

"No," he clarified. "Once we got up and we got ready to head back to our lives, I got hit with this wave of anxiety. I was going to tell you about it then and there but we had to make checkout time and then it was like I lost the moment and I..." Keith looked at me very solemnly. For someone who always projected confidence, I had never seen him this rattled. "I haven't told many people about this. But I think you have a right to know, and...it's not something I could say over the phone or on Skype."

I took his hand. It was what instinct demanded. Ironically, we hadn't held hands up until this point. I nodded almost imperceptibly to encourage him.

Privacy and decorum dictate that I can't go into full detail with you here. But the gist of it was, when he was in high school, an older man he had trusted forced himself on him.

And now things made sense that didn't before.

No wonder Keith had closed off. He said it might not have mattered before whether or not I knew. But we'd been getting closer, and instead of feeling safer the discomfort had been growing the more we got to know each other, especially once we tiptoed beyond our platonic boundaries by cuddling. He noted how weird it had been that he had been able to avoid the topic with the other guys he'd dated and with the few one-nighters he'd had; he supposed it was because no vulnerability had been required then. But something about the growing connection between us had put a magnifying glass on it all for him.

"I know we talked about communicating when stuff came up," Keith recognized. "It just got more awkward the more I put it off. But I'm communicating now, I hope. I'm getting better?" he asked with the hint of a smile.

I squeezed his hand, which had never let go of mine. "You are. I mean, you didn't ghost me. And hell, you invited me here."

"I really wanted to see you again. And I'm sorry about last night. I had every intention of cuddling with you. It's just that when I saw you, I realized how much I had let everything build up, and I was afraid if I let you that physically close to me you'd sense it instantly. That's why I banished you to the couch."

"Well...if it's any consolation...that's a damn comfortable couch. Come here."

I pulled him close; his head rested on my shoulder as I put my arms around him. Somehow that was even more beautiful than the rustling greenery above us and the sparkly stream trickling below us.

"Thank you for trusting me enough to tell me. You know, it's true what they say: everything goes back to childhood. That's been my experience, anyway."

"Truer words, Brody."

"And this might seem hollow, but...I'm sorry that man did that to you. It pisses me off to think anyone would hurt you like that."

Keith kissed my neck. "Well, if we do choose to take things to the next level one day, I just wanted you to know so there won't be any surprises when you end 'the drought'."

Oh, that. Shit. In this spirit of honesty and sincerity, I

knew I needed to say something. But it just didn't seem like the right time. I didn't think he would really care that I'd slept with someone. There was just a peripheral component that admission would ultimately bring up and it had a lot to do with why I hadn't gone to bed with Keith in Salt Lake. Not the only reason, but a big one. Well, maybe not that big.

You might think our having gotten so serious might have cast a pall on the rest of the afternoon and the evening. But it didn't. If anything, it lightened things up. Keith was visibly relieved and went out of his way to assure me there would be cuddling tonight in abundance. But first he wanted to take me on a tour of Bozeman and surrounding areas. We saw sprawling ranches and abandoned still-standing brick structures from the Gold Rush era and the myriad of cabin-inspired homes that got more prominent the closer you got to downtown. It was dark by the time we strolled down Main, which was liberally strung with lights and gave the impression the Milky Way had come down to street level. And then, Keith surprised me by holding my hand, right there on the avenue, as we walked.

I thought we might have dinner at one of these quaint little cafés or one of the butch-as-hell steak houses, but Keith had a different idea. He wanted to cook for me. We went back to his place, which was nestled in a blanket of trees on three out of four sides. Before we even got halfway up the driveway, he snapped his finger.

"Aw, man, I forgot dessert." He handed me a crumpled-up ten. "I really need to get dinner started or it'll be midnight before we eat. Would you mind running back down to the store for me? I'll text you the address; it's not far. Just pick out something chocolatey."

Getting sent on a mission to obtain chocolate is generally not something you have to talk me into. Not knowing what he was planning to make, I chose a nice cake that would pretty much go with anything. For a non-chain, small-town grocery, there was a rather diverse selection.

When I got back, I could see from outside he'd closed his curtains. As he'd told me to let myself in, I did so and I just stood there holding the cake in complete awe.

He'd lit what seemed like a hundred candles and turned his dining room into an Italian *ristorante*. He emerged from the kitchen all smiles.

"Um, you've gone pyro?" I grinned.

"Not pyro – Mario. My cooking's not gonna meet his standards, but we try."

"Well, what do you know," I sighed contently. "Casper the Friendly Ghost is a hopeless romantic."

"Nah, just hopeless. That cake looks good – why don't you pop it in the refrigerator until the time comes?"

He had stuff on every burner simmering and bubbling. The smell was intoxicating. "You mean to say you did all this just while I was at the store."

"Actually, I did a lot of the prep work before you got here yesterday. Hey, I figured if you ditched me I'd have twice as much food for tomorrow," he winked.

He started whistling an off-key but impossibly endearing version of *Bella Notte* while I opened his fridge and reached down to the bottom shelf to deposit the cake. There was already one there, and nicer than the one I'd gotten. That little shit. He had purposely gotten me out of the house so he could create a romantic setting for me.

I walked up behind him while he was stirring his sauce and clasped my arms around his waist. "You goofball," I whispered tenderly, kissing his ear as an accentuation.

I can't tell you how freeing it felt to be able to tap into that romantic part of myself again. I did remember given our history and just by way of the odds that this might not end up actually going anywhere. It was something I'd chewed on all the way back down the mountain and throughout the day after Keith had told me his secret. I might be letting myself in for another world of hurt if I finally and totally let my defenses down. Was I ready for that?

You know what I decided? Go for it. I had gotten another chance, not just with Keith but for love itself. And if the whole thing fell down around me again, I was going to enjoy and embrace as much of it as I could for as long as I could. Maybe that's what all that opening your heart stuff was about.

Oh, my God, it was so funny. At one point during dinner Keith suggested we try reenacting that spaghetti noodle shtick from *The Lady and the Tramp*. And it would have worked, too, if I hadn't stuck my elbow right in the middle of my plate reaching over to him before our lips could have met. We simply howled over that one.

Over dessert – we had decided to sample both cakes because we could – Keith brought out some photo albums. Inside were slightly yellowed, delicate images of a wonderfully dorky kid. Him. "You did say back at Redding – rather adamantly, as I recall – that you wanted to know more about my childhood."

He just kept on amazing me. "Do you remember everything I yell at you?" I quipped.

I was struck by one particular photo. Him at around eight, he said, proudly holding up a drawing that may not have been as polished as his current work, but absolutely showed the promise he would soon fulfill. "I still can't get over how talented you are," I marveled. "It's not just the mastery but the love that goes into every single line. Boy Keith clearly already had it."

"Your talent's nothing to sneeze at, either, you know. And not just your writing, although there's no mistaking your voice and your finesse. There's another talent you have that exhilarates me."

When his lips met mine again, it was like...forget it, I was going to say something totally cheesy. Suffice it to say it felt so right, and I hadn't until now allowed myself to acknowledge how much I'd missed him all those months that were just a bad memory now. There were no tears this time. And there was more want in our kisses. I was glad we'd moved over to the couch before it became evident I wasn't going to be able to stand up.

Things got more exploratory. Buttons became undone. I did grimace for a moment when his hand grazed the inside of my shirt. "I'm sorry the gym hasn't fulfilled its promise of a better body in twelve weeks..." I heaved self-deprecatingly.

"Surely you don't think I care about that."

Oh, man, he was so beautiful. I debated with myself how far to let things go, considering what he'd shared with me that afternoon and the remaining sins of omission I had made. When I realized his chest hair was tickling my nose, I had to summon everything in me to pull myself away from them.

"If I don't stop, I know I'm gonna pick you up and carry you into that bedroom. I may drop you before we get there, but I'll do it."

Keith was catching his own breath. "You think we should stop, then?" I briefly closed my eyes. "Because of what I told you in the woods?"

I instantly regained consciousness. "Oh, no. Not at all. It's just...all right. I have something to tell you, too. Um..." Maybe I could do this by first peeling away the top layer of the onion. "'The drought' has been over for a while."

"Oh. Really?"

"It was one of the dudes I went out with when you and I were just beginning to really become friends and anything happening between us didn't seem like even a remote possibility. What can I say...I often felt like I was being groomed for a monastery, but joining one wasn't on my to-do list."

"Is that what you're worried about?" Keith ruffled my curls. "Listen, at our age, neither of us are virgins. It's not like I didn't partake while we were out of touch."

I wondered when I was going to mature out of admissions like that bothering me. After all, he wasn't wrong. "Well, yeah...we're grown-ups. Needs and all. I just have met enough gay guys who feel compelled to talk about their sexual conquests and what they did and how long they did it. I'm not one of those."

"I'd never think you were."

"And you know, that night might have ended 'the drought' for sheer need, but it didn't really feel right, either."

"I know what you mean. Sex is great! I just found, even with the fellows I was dating when I met you, that something was missing. I dunno...maybe I've been looking for something out of this world."

We let a few moments pass in quiet. Then I indicated myself. "Buzzkill, huh?

"Oh, I have no intention of letting that be our last kiss for the night. I'm not sure I could go further than that given what you learned about me today – although I have to say I am feeling *very* comfortable with you. We can revert to a more PG-rated make-out session if you'd rather wait on the unrated director's cut."

"I..." I felt comfortable with him, too. It was me I wasn't feeling comfortable with. I had to tell him the rest of it. How unfair and cowardly was it to hold back when he had shared one of the most painful memories of his life with me? This wasn't anywhere near on par with that! But I couldn't force it out of my mouth. Instead I lied by telling a different truth. "I always rushed into sex when I was younger. I guess I had a tendency to mistake mens' lust for affection, which is what I really wanted. I think you're really special. And as fairy-tale as this is going to sound, I want our first time to be special, too."

"Don't say 'fairy'," Keith smirked. He held me firmly against him and yes, inevitably we got back to that huggin' and kissin' I didn't need to dream about anymore. Though this time our hands stayed (mostly) within respectable areas.

At one point before bed we put our heads together to suss out a time for a third date. This time he would be making the trip to see me in Reno, which he felt was only fair. I had no argument; there were a bunch of local landmarks and scenic superlatives I wanted to show him. We marked off a mutually workable schedule. I would have two and a half weeks to bite my own bullet. Maybe what I had to say wasn't going to be a dealbreaker. For some guys, it would be. Yes, I'd been hypocritical, asking him to communicate his fears to me and then not doing the same myself, at least, not in total. We had nearly made love and if we were going to have any intimacy at all, I was going to have to be as transparent with him as he had been with me.

17

THAT TWO AND A half weeks whizzed by. And no wonder. I had what I had decided would be an aliens-as-an-allegory-for-the-current-state-of-the-country sequel to work on, and Keith had back-to-back comic cons to squeeze in. However, something had definitely shifted. In the days following our first kiss in San Francisco, he'd do a con and basically disappear. Now he was still busy – and having worked a table with him, I knew how much – but he texted me in between. Maybe one or two lines as per usual, but they were much more meaningful lines. And he was much better about charging his phone.

One night he surprised me by calling from his hotel room. He sounded so exhausted, poor guy. He needed to get a commission done before he flew home the next day. I let him know how much I appreciated him picking up the phone when he had work to do. Positive reinforcement, right?

I tried to be better, too, by asking about his kids. It was at times habit for me to only think of his world as him. Claudia and Joseph were well, and Keith noted that he'd be spending the day with them before heading over to see me.

"They probably get their stubbornness more from me than they do their mother," he laughed. "But what a dull existence it would be without them."

I was curious and I hoped I wasn't overstepping. "You know, now knowing what happened to you as a teenager...do you think that's why you married a woman? As a reaction to that?"

Silence for a moment. Reflection or offense?

"Armchair psychiatrist 'til the end, eh?" Keith said. But there was no offense in his voice. "I've wondered about that sometimes. Maybe in part. Certainly such an introduction to being gay could have turned me off from men and created a fear of intimacy. I think it was also growing up in the time I did, living in non-cosmopolitan towns like the one I settled down in. My journey took what it took, I guess. I got Joe and Claudia out of the deal, though. So I'm not complaining."

"I'd love to meet them someday" came rushing out before I could stop it.

"Stranger things have happened," came his fond response. "Hey...I miss you, Brody."

It was like he had just articulated everything I was feeling in that moment. "I miss you, too."

So, the day came he would be driving down to my house. A house I'd had to do a bit of the Flight of the Bumblebee to get into some kind of presentable order. Tidiness is not my strong suit, especially when I get busy with creative work – housework just falls by the wayside. I also wanted to pull together some romantic ambience of my own. I couldn't believe I finally got to do this. I had daydreamed and nightdreamed about having him over in the days before things fell apart, and now I was getting that chance.

As with when I'd arrived in Bozeman, he kind of limped up the doorstep after spending all day in his car. I thought he might like to relax, so I ordered in a nice chicken dinner and popped in one of my favorite movies, which I knew he hadn't seen. The snuggling we'd begun during the flick continued on after the end credits rolled and the DVD menu looped. The kisses were sleepy but affectionate. It was one of those cute moments where I had to wake him up to put him to bed. I finally had a man in it, and not any man off a dating app. Keith Kirby. The man I'd tried so hard to forget about. As if that had been possible.

The fog I usually labor under in the morning seemed replaced by an eagerness to show Keith where I lived. You may have heard Reno is quite the tourist attraction for gamblers, but there was so much vibrance in its natural surroundings. Keith said he could understand why I'd chosen to live there after my first book broke through.

We drove a lot, with me rediscovering a lot of sights through his eyes, places I had learned to take for granted during my years there. We held hands almost constantly. There were the not-so-stolen looks. Our interaction was different somehow, though I stopped myself from delving too deeply into why. By the way, my heart wasn't just open here, it was downright tingly.

As with his talent for drawing, I also didn't share Keith's talent for cooking, so I compensated by taking him to my favorite restaurant. I knew the owner, which worked in my favor, since it allowed me a little creative control over the evening. We were seated in a cozy little booth that was partitioned off in a way you couldn't see the rest of the patrons. And I'd made certain suggestions regarding music.

I excused myself to the washroom, but I didn't require a meeting with Mother Nature. I wanted to retrieve something I'd had delivered to the restaurant. I returned to our table with my hands firmly clasped behind my back.

"What, did you lose your arms?" Keith chuckled.

I made a dramatic gesture out of placing fourteen yellow roses in front of him.

"What's this?" he beamed.

"Our appetizer," I snarked as I sat down. "No, seriously, we already covered the fear of intimacy part – this takes care of the fourteen and the yellow."

"They're beautiful." Keith leaned over to kiss me his thanks. "And the scent..." Then he got the most comical look on his face. "Do you remember everything I blurt out at you while I'm in disguise?"

"Only because of the ginkgo," I jested.

I'd supped at this eatery any number of times, but I couldn't remember having enjoyed it so much. As I drove us home, I knew what the night could bring. There wasn't going to be any way around what I needed to face if I wanted to meet Keith's honesty about his teenage experience, which he was braving in pursuing this with me. I had to wipe my own slate clean.

Speaking of slates, he asked me the strangest thing when we got in the door. He'd fallen a little behind on his commission work during the comic cons and he wanted to know if it would be okay if he finished it up before we continued our evening. Not exactly the direction I thought things were headed in, but our work had to get done. So I set him up in the living room and read a book in my office. I'd rather write books, but reading is a luxury I hadn't afforded myself for a while.

I peeked out and asked if he'd like some coffee or something. He settled on tea so I made some for both of us, bringing him a steaming mug. He covered his sketch almost conspiratorially.

"It's not done yet. I just need another half an hour or so."

And that I gave him, feeling a bit like the romantic edge had been taken off the evening. Just when I got to the point I found myself re-reading the same sentences two or three times, I heard a gentle knock on my office's door frame. "Sorry to keep you waiting so long," Keith said sheepishly. "I just really needed to get that done."

"I understand," I said as I got up to meet him. "More Phoenix-related stuff or is this one of your personal ventures?"

"Definitely personal. It's kind of a storyboard for a new project I've been thinking a lot about undertaking. But you know, I could use a fresh eye. Maybe have a look and tell me your thoughts?"

We walked to the living room and he handed me his sketchpad. This was neat, getting to see a new work of his at the development stage. I took the pad from him and flipped its cover. What was underneath it I was in no way ready for.

It was a beautiful rendition...of us. He had captured our likenesses perfectly, using vivid colors to accentuate them. His avatar faced mine as if they were looking into each other's eyes, and a speech balloon appeared beside his two-dimensional mouth.

It said, *I'm falling in love with you.*

If there was any oxygen in the room, I wasn't getting any of it. I looked up at his smiling, bearded face. It was like all the matter in the universe was stuck in my throat.

"Wow, I've got the writer at a loss for words," Keith commented. "What are your impressions? This an enterprise worth pursuing?"

I gently put his sketchpad down on my coffee table. He actually looked a little worried.

I punched something up on my laptop, which I had plugged speakers into the night before. I hadn't expected to play this song, but it seemed only fitting for the occasion.

I approached him during the intro's high strings and held my hand out to him. "May I?"

I don't know if he had ever slow danced with a guy before; I knew I hadn't, but it was something I had always wanted to do and never gotten to. So admittedly we were a little unsure of whose hands were supposed to go where, etc. But they found their places as the vocals began.

At last...my love has come along...

Keith softly chuckled at the lyric. But he could tell Etta James was singing my answer. And there we swayed in my living room for those three minutes of wonderful eternity, circling ever so slowly. And I'm not afraid to admit it – I did cry a little bit. But there was no question whether the few teardrops were happy or sad. He wiped them away gently and we just gazed into each other's eyes with a love that no longer had to be run from or denied.

The song came to an end but our swaying didn't, at least not at first. When it did, I gave him a look. "You're sure about this."

Keith caressed my face lovingly. "When someone shows you who they are...believe them the first time."

It stung a little remembering I had used that Maya Angelou quote to flame him in Redding – but what a romantic way to turn it around on me. And actually, I hadn't been wrong then. The man standing in front of me, the man who had just professed his love to me, the man who was confirming it with the tenderest kiss we'd shared yet was exactly who he was when I'd first met him. That's why I had literally left my heart in San Francisco, and why it had hurt so much to think he was gone from my life. Because I had believed who he was...it was just his actions hadn't matched up to it. Until now.

Our kissing slowly became more passionate. I knew what he wanted and I knew what I wanted. It felt like the time, as if it would affirm the feelings I could now be certain we both had. I stalled a little bit, in part to make the mutual seduction last longer. But also...my own moment of truth had arrived. I don't know why I kept making such a big deal out of it to myself. Or, in this case...

We had slowly travelled over to my bedroom, lips constantly joined. From the unmistakable fragrance I didn't need to open my eyes to know Keith had placed his now-vased roses in there during his artistic subterfuge. By now we were taking turns sucking on each others' tongues. He reached for my pants...

I laid a hand on his hand. "Wait."

I could tell Keith didn't want to stop the train now that it was chugging down the track. But I could also tell he cared more about me than his hormones. "Is something wrong?"

"I think only you're only going to be able to determine that."

"What do you mean?"

God, Brody, stop being such a drama queen and just say it. Or maybe it would be better if my tell ended up being a show-and-tell.

I felt scared and strangely defiant as I backed up, unbuttoned my own pants, and pulled them down around my thighs. "Here you see me as I really am. I can't help it; it's just, for all the gifts I've been blessed with, that isn't one of them."

Keith seemed a little confused by my fast-forward striptease.

Finally he said, "Did you really think that would matter to me?"

Some old hurt came up as I told him, "It mattered to my ex. He was definitely into size. In fact, that had a lot to do with why he insisted on an open relationship between us. He could get the emotional stuff from me but the Long Dong Silvers from other guys. I, uh, guess I developed a – ahem – little complex about it. And it's just one more reason for 'the drought'. You know how guys on apps are – the higher the number, the better."

Keith moved closer and gave my number a playful tug. "I like it because it's part of you. Average, maybe, but not little. I don't care that you don't look like you walked out of a Pornhub video. You have other things that make up for it. So many other things."

And then he got down in front of me and showed me how much he liked it. I felt like all however many millions or billions of nerve endings in my body were concentrated there. I had to slow him down a bit. "I should also mention," I confessed as I looked down at him, "I also have a what you might call a hair trigger on this gun."

He arched an eyebrow. "Then I'll take care to make sure it doesn't fire unless it's aimed at the right target."

Let's just say he wasn't only an artist when it came to drawing animated characters. Keith knew his way around three-dimensional anatomy and made it his mission to find every erogenous zone I had. For my part, all the passion that had come back to life in me after so many years made itself known; I was famished and I treated him like my own personal smorgasbörd. There wasn't a square inch of skin on either of us that didn't get explored with hands and lips and tongues. And all the while, everything in me knew that *this* was making love. It wasn't just a fuck, could never be, not now with each of us having admitted feelings for each other.

The best part of it wasn't even the sex. There wasn't just grunting and groaning going on. At times we got silly and we laughed a lot. For however Keith might be afraid of intimacy, he was sure giving it a chance. That just made me feel even closer to him.

And okay, one last true confession for you. I let him do...that, too. I know it's kind of par for the course for most gay guys one way or the other, but I had always had a level of unease about the few times I'd done it. Not with Keith. That act was as loving as all the others that had preceded it. For the very first time (ahem), it had felt right. So right. Like he was Cinderella's foot and I was the glass slipper.

Someday, my prince will – oh, sorry, different Disney movie. And my prince did, as did I, but only after he skillfully allayed my worry about it happening too quickly. I never wanted him out of me. But as much as I was enjoying looking up at him with his sweat dripping on my face, after ten minutes or so I started to feel like my legs were going to permanently lock in that position so I reluctantly disjoined us and his protection came off (yes, safe sex, thank you very much! And damn right we talked about HIV statuses first). We pulled the crumpled sheets up over us and wrapped our arms around each other, eventually sticking together from that special kind of glue he had coaxed out of me.

"Thank you, my sweet Brody," Keith said, giving me a kiss as sweet. I looked at him mock-incredulously.

"Thank *me*? Thank *you*. Being with you this way was only a year and a half in coming. Um...so to speak."

We lay there in my bed, playing with each other's hair, staring at each other for who knows how many minutes. Then I had to suppress a sudden urge to laugh.

"Alllll riiiight," came Keith's sing-song response. "What's going through that endlessly creative brain of yours?" He really did know me pretty well at this point.

"Oh, it's nothing. This quote decided to pop into my head." I did my best Kim Basinger. "'I just gotta know – are we gonna try to love each other?'"

Keith's eyes widened in recognition. "Ah! *Batman*, the 1989 version with Michael Keaton."

I tried to give him my most serious "Duh!" reaction, but my giggle ruined it. "No – *Batman*, the 1989 Prince soundtrack. Oh, dear. There's so much I'm going to have to teach you."

Keith smiled that smile that still went right through me. "I hope so."

Yes, I was in love with Keith Kirby. I could finally say it. Maybe I always had been; maybe it really had been love at first sight for me. Despite having spent so much time chastising myself for falling too fast, maybe it was just okay that that's how my heart worked.

Even I wasn't juvenile enough to expect some happily-ever-after. We still each had our own psychological and mental stuff to deal with, issues that could come into conflict down the road. Road! There was still the matter of several hundred miles of it stretching between our homes, and I had no idea how we were going to work that one out.

And of course being in an actual relationship was way different than fantasizing about someone or even "merely" falling in love with them. I was going to have to work on unblurring the lines with that one.

But it was like Vicki Vale said. All we could do was try to love each other. Tonight was a good start. Because we'd discovered there was love between us to try *with*. That's all anybody can ask for, really.

As we fell asleep in each others' arms, as what emanated from our open hearts seemed to fill the entire room as much as did the scent of fourteen yellow roses,

I thought about everything that had led us here and the life-altering sketch that sat on my coffee table, waiting to be framed. And it occurred to me – in both cases – that sometimes before we can appreciate things, they really do have to be drawn out.

www.ingramcontent.com/pod-product-compliance
Lightning Source LLC
LaVergne TN
LVHW030922080826
845145LV00013B/3011